Burgess

Rigby Brothers, Volume 2

S L Davies

Published by S L Davies, 2022.

BURGESS

First edition. September 14, 2022.

Copyright © 2022 S L Davies.

ISBN: 979-8215163139

Written by S L Davies.

Prologue

Caspian

"Pull back, pull back," the captain roared through the radio. I turned to see what the panic was. The house was already an inferno when we arrived. A mother had been screaming about her children that were stuck in the house. We'd gone in without a second thought. This was our job.

As I looked back towards the captain, I saw the source of his panic. One of the beams that stood between me and the rest of my team was about to collapse. I turned and ran for the door. A loud crack sounded. I looked up at the last minute just in time to see the beam come crashing down on top of me.

"Caspian," I heard someone shout, but through the ringing in my ears and the searing pain in my body, I wasn't able to decipher who it was.

It was beeping that I woke up to. My eye blinked open. Confusion settled in my mind. *What the hell had happened?* I cast my mind back. I remembered entering the burning building. Looking for two children. Then the beam. The pain.

The pain that was enveloping my entire body at that moment. So much fucking pain. I'd sunk back into the darkness. Every time I woke the pain was unbearable. The drugs the doctors kept me pumped with, helped slightly. But they also slowed down my natural healing.

It took a month before my healing finally took away the pain in my body. The scarring was another matter. My supernatural healing was never able to fix it. One side of my face was completely marred. The scars were still pink and bubbled as if the right side of my face had completely melted. The scarring went down over my neck, back, shoulder, arm, and chest.

Doctors had said I was lucky. I lost my right eye, and the scarring made my voice scratchy. My lungs had been filled with soot, but the doctors said there weren't many people that survived such damage. I still didn't see how that was lucky. I had to now live like a freak.

I saw the way that my teammates from Lalbert Fire looked at me when they came in. There was always a mix of pity and disgust. I wanted to hide away. I was just glad that I lived in the forest and didn't have to venture into town for much. I'd been pretty much self-sufficient since I built my house. My dream was one day to get off the grid and live completely self-sufficiently. Now my goals became a necessity.

"This is a support group for service people who have been injured on the job. I'd like you to attend. I think you will get a lot out of it," Dr. Carlisle said as she handed me a brochure. For some reason, I needed a psychiatrist now. Dr. Carlisle was nice, and she was patient with me, but seriously, there was nothing wrong with my head. It was my skin that was scarred, not my brain.

"Really? Is sitting around crying as a group really going to do anything to change the way I look?" I growled.

Dr. Carlisle rolled her eyes. As well as being incessantly patient she also didn't put up with my bullshit. I'd never been this growly alpha before. I'd always been happy and easy-going. Most fae were. But since this accident, I felt like it had transformed me into a bear shifter.

"It won't take the scars away, no," Dr. Carlisle said with a sigh. "But what it will do is introduce you to other men and women who have been through similar trauma. They have had to learn to live with similar injuries and understand what they are going through. It will arm you with knowledge. And you never know, you might actually like some people there."

I rolled my one good eye and sighed. "Yeah alright. I'll try to get there."

"I suppose that is all I can ask," Dr. Carlisle said. I could see from the look on her face that she would have liked more of a commitment from me, but it was the best she was going to get.

I'd tossed the brochure on my coffee table the minute I got home and didn't bother picking it up again. It was something I would think about later. All I wanted to do was to close the curtains, close my eye and sleep until this nightmare was over.

But the nightmare wasn't going to go away. It took two weeks of ignoring everything and everyone before I finally glanced at the brochure that sat on a dusty coffee table. I picked it up and glanced at the double-sided printed paper. It talked about support, friendship, and understanding. I sighed and picked up my phone that was still sitting where I'd left it. After powering it up, I wasn't surprised to see several missed calls and texts from different friends that I'd made through the years.

They couldn't have missed me too much. None of them came and knocked on my door. It was all just talk. The odd message to make themselves feel better. I scoffed and looked back at the brochure before typing the number into the screen of my phone.

"Hello, this is Tally," a pretty little voice sounded through the phone.

"Um, yeah, hi, Tally. My name is Caspian Lyons. I was given a brochure to the support group. I just need some information on what I need to do."

"Caspian, it's wonderful to talk to you. Dr. Carlisle let me know that you might call. I'm glad you did. We meet every Tuesday at the Methodist Church on Lalbert Street. Don't be fooled by the fact that we meet at the church, we aren't a religious group, we are just able to use their room for free," Tally said with a smile in her voice.

"And I just show up?" I asked.

"Yes. The meeting starts at six. But if you want to come a little bit early so that you can meet everyone, feel free to."

"Yeah alright. I'll try and get there on Tuesday then."

"That would be tonight," Tally said tenderly. I frowned and glanced at my phone. Realizing I'd lost track of time.

"Oh okay. Yeah. I'll try and get there tonight then."

"Alright, Caspian it will be good to meet you," Tally said before saying her goodbyes.

I leaned back in the chair and closed my eyes. I wondered if I really needed it. But what were the options? I could either go and meet people who understood what I was going through, or I could sit in my house alone feeling sorry for myself. Neither choice felt appealing to me.

Chapter One

B urgess
"Uncle Burgie I'm ready for my tattoo," Bear, my nephew called as he came running into the shop.

"Bear, stop running," March, his Papa yelled as the little bear shifter came running into the office where I was sitting doing some paperwork.

I was going to be spending the day babysitting my nephew Bear, my eldest Brother Asher's son, and his cousins Iver and McKenna. They all loved coming to Shifter Ink. Usually, they were able to con a few of us to give them tattoos. They were all drawn on with sharpies. March and Joachim would complain about what a bitch the sharpies were to wash off, but the kids loved their tattoos.

"Bear bug," I said with a grin as he rounded the corner with a piece of paper in his hand waving about wildly. "Did you design your tattoo?"

Bear nodded his head rapidly while looking up at me with big brown eyes. "I want a bear fighting with a sword," he said as he opened the piece of paper where sure enough there was a bear fighting with a sword drawn.

"Is this you?" I asked.

Bear grinned and nodded again. "Yep," he said popping the p.

I chuckled and glanced up at March who was waddling into the office. He was two months pregnant, but you'd swear he was about to drop any day. The doctors had been checking him a lot more closely after we nearly lost Bear when he was born.

"Are you sure it's okay to watch Bear while Asher and I go to see Dr. Osbourne?" March asked. From the look on his face, he was exhausted. Bear was a handful, that was for sure. He was a typical three-year-old boy. Full of life and energy.

"Of course. Take your time though, make sure Asher takes you out for some lunch or something too. You need a break."

March gave me a smile of appreciation. "Thanks, Burgess. It's been a hell of a week."

I chuckled. "Asher told me. I hear you lost two sadists at the club to mates."

March sighed and nodded. "Yeah. We've been trying to find others that can step up to do presentations. Asher has some in mind, but I don't know if they will work out or not. Time will tell, I guess. Hawke said that he was still willing to do some basic training sessions, using his mate, Jabari. But they've been pretty flat out with the Onyx Rebels. As has Freya and the Devil's Advocates."

"Yeah, I was talking to Anghus, and he was telling me all about the school they are starting to build."

March smiled and nodded. "It's really peaceful out there. Almost makes me want to pack up and live there. But then I think about living close to Donte," he replied with a laugh. Donte was March's brother-in-law. He and Asher hadn't seen eye to eye when they first met, but as far as I understood it, they had reached a truce.

"I'm not sure Bacchus would want Asher living out there anyway. Asher can be a bossy son of a bitch when he wants to," I laughed.

March smirked. "Just the way I like him," he said licking his lips causing me to bark out a laugh.

"Uncle Burgie, can I get my tattoo now?" Bear asked. He'd used up all his patience waiting for me and his father to stop talking.

I nodded my head and smiled. "Come on buddy, go and climb up on my station and I'll come and give you a tattoo then we are going back to Grandma and Pa's house to look after Iver and McKenna."

Bear's smile beamed as he nodded his head and dashed out of the office and to where my station was set up. I could hear my other tattooists greeting him as he entered the room. Shifter Ink was my pride and joy. I'd discovered that I loved art as a very young child. I'd thought I wanted to be an artist, but when I was sixteen, I apprenticed as a tattooist. After that, I found my passion.

"I've got some more art coming too," March said with a smile. He'd been painting large canvases for us since I first met him. We sold his artwork in the shop and so far, it was making him a pretty penny.

"Any more news from Chris about the gallery space?" I asked as I stood and started to head out to the main floor.

March nodded his head. "Early next year we've booked in for my first show."

"That's awesome man. When you have them, bring in flyers or whatever you're going to use to advertise, I'll plug it here at the studio."

March grinned and reached out to envelope me in a hug. "Thank you so much. You're awesome."

I chuckled and kissed my brother-in-law on the cheek. "Make sure you remember that when you're trying to wash sharpie off your kid later."

March groaned and shook his head, but I could see there was no anger in it. I waved goodbye to March and went over to where I kept my sharpies.

"Alright, sir, where are we tattooing you today?" I asked Bear who was already stripped of his shirt and laying on his stomach on my work bench.

"Back please Mr. Tattoo," he replied with a broad smile.

I sat down on my stool and set about working up a tattoo bear fighting with a sword.

Chapter Two

Caspian

"Are you actually going to talk today?" Macklin teased as we walked towards the Methodist church together.

It had been almost a year since the day of my accident. The scarring had settled and didn't cause me any more pain. The skin was taking some getting used to still. I had my mirrors covered in the house and didn't venture out except for my weekly therapy group.

Despite Macklin's teasing, I did interact occasionally. Macklin was an ex-soldier who'd got caught up in a bombing. Lost one of his eyes to shrapnel and all of his teammates. We'd become fast friends. Macklin was the only one that I invited into my home. He understood me. Over the year all my friends had dropped away. I didn't get any more phone calls or messages. Instead, it was radio silence. Not that I could overly blame them, there are only so many times their calls and texts go unanswered before they just give up.

"I'll talk when you do," I jibed back. Macklin and I were tarred with the same brush. We had both been proud men. Both alpha's and both felt invincible until the creator decided to humble our asses by causing damage to our bodies and minds.

Macklin chuckled and swung the front doors to the Methodist church open. I'd never admit it out loud, but these therapy group sessions had been a saving grace to me. After the first few months of the accident, I found myself lost, lonely and more than once I considered putting a bullet in my brain.

My friendship with Macklin helped and I liked to hope that maybe I helped him too. He'd been coming for several years more than I had, but it was still good to have someone that truly understands what it felt like to be on the front lines of a dangerous situation, only to have your life change in a moment.

"Macklin, Caspian, great to see you guys," Dr. Carlisle smiled as we approached. The fae doctor had also been a saving grace, even though I would deny it until I was blue in the face. "We have some new members joining us today."

I nodded my head and walked over to the table where the coffee and tea were laid out. After filling a cup of black coffee for myself and the overly sweetened and milky version for Macklin we took our seats.

"Alright, everyone is here. I'd like to take a moment to introduce myself to our new participants. My name is Dr. Lilibeth Carlisle. I am a certified psychiatrist with specialties in supernatural's and post-traumatic stress disorder. I'd like it if we could please go around the room and introduce ourselves. Let's start with our new members?"

A small man that was sitting in a wheelchair and missing both of his legs smiled. "Hello, my name is Jonathon. I am a warthog shifter. I was in a car accident five months ago and lost both of my legs. It's nice to see you all."

Dr. Carlisle smiled and thanked Jonathon for his participation before turning to the lady that sat next to him. In comparison, she was completely different. She held her head high and her red eyes shone with what appeared to be anger.

"My name is Magda," she started with a very thick European accent. "I was abducted as a child and tortured. As a result, I have burns to seventy percent of my body."

I winced at the story. I had heard about the different breeding facilities that were out there. Ones that took children to breed them for either science experiments, their own sick pleasure or to make them fight.

"Thank you, Magda. I'm glad you felt comfortable to attend tonight," Dr. Carlisle said before she turned to me.

I raised my hand and smiled before ducking my head. "My name is Caspian. I was a firefighter until a year ago when a beam fell from a building trapping me beneath it. The scars are from the fire."

Dr. Carlisle smiled again. "Thank you, Caspian."

"Hey, I'm Macklin. I was in the army and involved in an IED attack on our vehicles. As a result, I lost one of my eyes and have some scarring dotted across my body."

The introductions continued until everyone in the room had given their name and a brief description of how we became to be the freaks we now were. I know that wasn't fair. I didn't actually view anyone else as a freak. Just myself.

I tuned out as Dr. Carlisle started to talk about what our victories were during the week and what we needed to overcome. I never took any notice of this part. I didn't take part in it anyway, so what was the point. If it hadn't been for Macklin being here every week, I probably wouldn't have stuck at coming. But as it stood, his friendship and seeing him every week was my highlight.

"Caspian? How about you tell us something good about your week?" Dr. Carlisle asked breaking into my thoughts.

I bit down on my lips to stop the groan from escaping that I felt building inside me. I hated being asked to speak. But she tried it every few weeks. With a sigh, I shrugged my shoulders.

"My tomatoes started fruiting," I said with a quirk of my lips.

I swore I could almost see Dr. Carlisle roll her eyes. I knew that it wasn't what she was looking for, but I hated that everyone needed to know my business.

"Well, I'm glad to hear it. Maybe you could bring some in when they are ready, I'd like to try one. But did anything happen for you personally, something that maybe challenged you that you were able to overcome?"

I shook my head. "Nothing that I could think of."

Dr. Carlisle raised her eyebrow and shot me a glare. It was as if she thought I was purposely trying to be obtuse. But I really wasn't. It's just that nothing ever happened in my life. I lived it, I got up every morning did my chores then crashed in the afternoon in front of the television before it was time to do it all over again.

"I know that you struggle to look in mirrors, have you successfully been able to achieve that yet?" Dr. Carlisle asked, playing dirty. That was something I had admitted to her in our one on one session.

I was miffed that she would bring it up in the group therapy. I narrowed my eye and felt myself wanting to growl.

"Yes, Dr. Carlisle I sat with the mirror between my legs and looked at my vagina," I spat before crossing my arms over my chest. Macklin snorted a laugh beside me. Dr. Carlisle's face blazed red, and she nodded her head.

"Robert? What about you?" she said moving on to her next victim.

Macklin was still chuckling beside me as the conversation went on. This was the kind of shit reason why I hadn't wanted to attend the fucking therapy sessions in the first place. If she was going to start bringing up bullshit that I admitted in our one on one sessions then fuck her. I sat back in my seat and seethed for the rest of the evening.

Once it was time to end the meeting, I stood up ready to dash out of the building. I didn't have time for this bullshit.

"Caspian, can I speak to you a moment?" Dr. Carlisle called before I had a chance to reach the doors and my freedom. I growled in my throat and turned to face the doctor. "Caspian, I want to apologize, I was out of line for asking you about the mirrors."

"Yes, you were," I growled.

Dr. Carlisle nodded and sighed. "I'm sorry. I hope to see you next week for our appointment."

I hummed but didn't give the doctor a proper answer before turning and stalking out of the church building and into the cool night air towards the waiting uber.

Chapter Three

Burgess

"Come around on the weekend," Mama said down the phone as I sat in my living room with my feet kicked up. We were going to be celebrating the birth of our latest family member. A spider shifter omega called Ivy. From all accounts, she was gorgeous and tiny.

"I will. What do you want me to bring?" I asked.

"Oh, can you make that beautiful pumpkin salad you make? March will love that," Mama replied.

I chuckled. She was always trying to find new and exciting vegetarian dishes to serve March. What she didn't realize was that he was happy just being loved on. He didn't care about the food. But this was my Mama's love language. Food.

"Sure thing, anything else?" I questioned.

"No sweetheart, I think that should be enough now."

After a few more minutes of small talk, Mama said her goodbyes and I stretched out on the couch. I probably should have been drawing up more designs for the shop window, but I'd been so busy the last week or two that I just didn't have the energy. While March was in the hospital with Ivy, I had been looking after Bear. I didn't mind, but he had a lot of energy so everything I needed to do for the shop had to wait until he was in bed. That meant I didn't get to bed until well after midnight and then was up at the crack of dawn again with him.

Add on top of that Iver and McKenna, while Anghus and Joachim worked on the finishing touches for the school, and it was safe to say I was thoroughly exhausted and felt like I could sleep for a week. The television was playing softly, and I was drifting on and off when my phone startled me with a ring.

Glancing at the screen I was surprised to see that it was Macklin calling. It wasn't like my brother to make a general call, so something had to be wrong.

"Hey Mack, you alright?" I asked.

Macklin chuckled. "Yeah, I'm fine. I swear you all worry too much."

"Well, it's not like you call us just to say hello."

Macklin hummed. "Yeah, I need to change that."

Macklin had been through a lot. When we were growing up, he was the life of the party. A real social butterfly. None of us were surprised when he joined the army. But his time there had been horrible. When he was deployed, we were all worried about what it would do to him.

When we got word that he'd been in an attack with an IED, panic had rippled through the family. What we never expected was to get back a shell of a man. He was broken. Not just physically but emotionally and mentally. For the first twelve months, he had extremely violent flashbacks and nightmares.

I remember coming into the house one day to see my father and Asher having him pinned to the ground while he screamed bloody murder. It was the most terrifying thing I'd ever seen. However, after countless doctors' appointments and therapy they were able to stabilize him with medication.

It didn't mean that he ever went back to the guy he was before his time in the middle east, but he was at least calm, and we didn't fear him hurting someone he loved during a flashback.

"We get it, man. So, what's up?" I said.

"I wanted to ask you a question about a tattoo," he replied.

I sat up on the couch and kicked my feet up onto the coffee table in front of me. "Oh yeah, thinking about getting some more ink?"

"One day, but this isn't for me. I have a friend. He was a firefighter; Jericho knows him too. Anyway, he was burned a year ago really bad and has some massive scarring. He is really self-conscious about it, and I suggested to him a tattoo to cover some of the worst areas. I told him that you were an artist and specialized in supernaturals. But I wasn't sure whether you could tattoo over the scarring."

I hummed. "Yeah, it can be tricky. Some scarring is so thick that it won't take the ink very well. Not to mention it can be very painful to tattoo over scar tissue. I'm happy to check it out though. Without seeing him I wouldn't be able to tell you for sure whether he would be suitable. There is some new ink out, it's specifically designed for shifters. It has a compound in it so that the tattoos are visible even in their shifted form. I've found that it's the best ink when dealing with scars too."

"Caspian is fae. But that sounds like it could be promising."

"Where are the scars and how bad are we talking?" I asked.

"All over the right side of his face and down over his chest, back, and arm. I haven't seen what's under his shirt, so I can't tell you how bad it gets, but the scarring on his face is pretty severe."

I winced and hummed. "Yeah, it might not be practical. But like I said I'm willing to have a look. It all depends on how deep the scar tissue is, how thick it is. But I'm willing to check it out. I won't be charging him for the tattoo."

"Thanks, man, I'll let him know. There is just one other thing about it though."

"What's that?"

"He won't come into the shop. You'd have to go to him. He has become a bit of a shut-in as a result of the accident."

"Ah, I see. How did you meet him then?"

"Through the group therapy. It's the only place he goes."

"Alright, well talk to him, tell him that I'm willing to check it out. If he is comfortable with me coming into his space, then I'm happy to do that. We won't tattoo him straight away as I'd have to work on a design and everything first."

"Awesome, thanks bro," Macklin said with an obvious smile in his voice.

"No worries. I'll see you on the weekend and talk more to you about it."

Macklin said his goodbyes and ended the call. Images of designs I could draw up for Caspian floated through my head. He didn't sound familiar to me. I'd thought I'd met all of Jericho's teammates, but I didn't remember a Caspian.

Chapter Four

C aspian

It was Macklin that first brought up the idea of getting tattoos. I'd not really given it a thought, but Macklin said that his brother was a great tattoo artist and would know whether my scars could be covered. The more he talked about it, the more interested I became.

When I'd researched whether burn scars could even be tattooed over, there was a plethora of information. From what I could tell, most tattoo artists that commented on the subject said the scars could be tattooed over. However, it was painful and tricky. It would take a great tattoo artist to be able to work the scars into a design that didn't make it look like a nasty cover-up job.

I'd looked up Shifter Ink and checked out their work. Burgess, Macklin's brother had a lot of talent that was for sure. He specialized in realistic tattoos. And specialized in working with supernatural bodies. Most of his artists had a lot of talent. I was impressed by what I saw.

When Macklin rang to tell me that he'd spoken to his brother and Burgess was willing to come out to the house to meet with me I was nervous, to say the least. Over the last year, it had only been Macklin that had come into my house. This was ironic, considering before the accident, my house had been a place to socialize and spend time with friends.

I didn't have any family that I knew. But I'd built a strong friend base. It mustn't have been too strong though, seeing as the only one left was Macklin and I met him after the accident. Even his brother Jericho, who had been one of my teammates, no longer called. He usually just sent a message through Macklin to say hello.

I'd spent the morning cleaning, making sure everything was dusted and tidy. I didn't want Burgess to think I lived like a pig. Not that I should be worried, I was pretty clean anyway. But I didn't think Burgess would care. From what Macklin said, Burgess was one of the more laid-back brothers. An antelope omega.

The doorbell rang and I shook my hands nervously. Sucking in a deep breath I went to the front door and swung it open. Gasping at the sight in front of me. A beautiful man, with deep ginger hair and beard and the most beautiful hazel eyes, looked up at me with wide eyes.

"Holy shit," he whispered. "Mate."

My eyes widened and my mouth dropped open. There was no denying that scent that enveloped me. Burgess was my mate. A bubble of laughter rippled up through my chest and burst out of my lips. Soon I was doubled over laughing hysterically, tears ran from the corner of my eye.

I looked up at Burgess who was watching me with a slight frown on his face. I suppose I looked like a mad man. I shook my head and my laughter sobered.

"I'm sorry. I just never thought I would ever meet a mate. Not when I look like this," I said as I waved my hand over my face.

Burgess's lips quirked and he reached out a tender hand stroking his fingers down over the raised skin. He was the first person to touch my scars since the doctors. I gasped at the gentleness he caressed my skin with. I wanted to shrink away from this beautiful man that stood in front of me. But he held me captive. I couldn't move.

"Your scars add to your beauty," Burgess said quietly. "They speak of your life. They tell your story." I frowned but didn't say anything. Burgess blinked and looked up into my eyes. "I want you to be my mate."

I bit into my bottom lip and nodded my head. "Really?"

Burgess smiled. "Really."

I slowly let out a breath. *Could it really be that simple? I knew that for fated mates it was all about biology but was Burgess telling the truth when he said he wanted to be my mate?*

"Not just because you are fated to me?" I questioned.

Burgess smiled and took my hand in his. In his other hand, he held a bag. He skimmed his thumb over the back of my knuckles and looked deep into my eyes.

"I want you for you. I am attracted to you, despite the scars. I want you because Mother fate believed that we are destined to be a team. I want you because I see the beautiful man that is behind the scars. I can see into your soul and know that despite the pain you've been through, you are gentle."

My frown deepened and I shook my head. "How? How can you see all those things, just from looking at me?"

"I may only be an antelope shifter and not a mystical, but I still have supernatural power. My power is to see behind the walls that people build around them. It comes in handy. But it also allows me to see into you. The real you."

My mouth dropped open, and I stared at Burgess. "How? I don't understand."

"Supernatural's all have power. You do too. You just might not have taken the time to discover it yet."

I shook my head. I didn't know of any power that I had. I'd just always thought I was a fae with nothing special about me. I didn't grow up with parents. I grew up in the foster system, usually with humans. I attended a human school. I never learned about being supernatural. But what Burgess said, had me curious.

"Will you come inside?" I asked.

Burgess grinned. "I thought you'd never ask."

I chuckled and kept my hand in his as I led him over the threshold into the house and into my living room. I wanted to take him straight to the bedroom, but I wasn't sure what to do. I'd never been this nervous around a lover before. I almost felt like it was my first time all over again.

Chapter Five

Burgess

I didn't expect to be greeted by my mate when I turned up at Caspian's house. Macklin told me that since the accident he'd pretty much shut himself off from the world. He hated the way people looked at him and his scars. The first look at him told me why. The right side of his face was scarred terribly. It was impossible not to miss it. But it didn't take away from the fact that he was a beautiful man.

He stood just over six feet tall. Not much taller than me. He was thin but had defined muscles that I knew came from partly being fae but spending a lot of time outside working. His skin that wasn't scarred was tanned. His dark hair curled at his neck and his green eye held so much mystery.

We sat on the couch just looking at one another. I wasn't sure whether I should wait for him to make the first move. My heat was starting to set in, and I knew that if I didn't do something soon, I would be too far into heat that I wouldn't be able to enjoy the time. Slowly I leaned forward and skimmed my fingers up over Caspian's face. He hissed but it wasn't in pain, it was in shock that I was willing to touch the parts of him that he thought were ugly.

I moved slowly to give Caspian a chance to move away. He watched me with that one eye. I could see fear in him. He was terrified of being rejected. Since Bacchus and Anghus started working with the Onyx Rebels, I'd also been doing work with them. Working on the power that was inside me. I was an antelope shifter, but I also had fae magic inside me. It allowed me to read inside what most people wanted to hide. Caspian was no different. The fear poured off him so strongly I could practically taste it.

Lightly I pressed my lips against his. Caspian's breath escaped him on a deep sigh. Pressing firmer against his mouth I swiped my tongue across his bottom lip, encouraging him to open his mouth. Caspian groaned and tentatively wound his arms around my waist, holding me tighter against him. My cock was throbbing in my jeans, and I could scent my arousal in the air.

Caspian groaned again and tangled his tongue with mine. Like his alpha finally got the message, he took over the kiss and tilted his head to make our kiss deeper. I inwardly smiled as I straddled his lap and tangled my fingers in the hair at the back of his neck. Rocking back and forth on Caspian's lap I was thrilled to feel him equally as hard. He wanted me just as much.

Caspian broke the kiss and looked up at me. He was still afraid, but the lust was taking over, which was exactly what I wanted. "It's been a long time since I've been with someone. Not since, well not since this," he said waving his hand over his face.

I nodded my head. "I want you Caspian. All of you. Scars and all."

Caspian's brow pulled into a warped frown. "Are you sure?"

"Absolutely."

He nodded as if making up his own mind. With ease, he lifted me into his arms, and I wound my legs around his waist as he carried me towards what I assumed was a bedroom. Caspian laid me out gently on the bed and then slowly lifted my shirt up and off my body. I lifted my arms so that he could easily slip it off my head.

He kneeled on the carpet and took one of my feet reverently in his hands and slipped my boot from my foot before doing the same with the other foot. Skimming his hands up over my jean-covered legs, he reached the waist band and unbuttoned my jeans, before sliding them down over my legs, leaving me in my boxers and socks. My boxers were tented with my excitement. I couldn't move. I silently watched as Caspian then took each sock off and laid it down over my boots. Finally, he reached for the waistband of my boxers, and I lifted my hips so that he could slide them down my legs easily. My cock bounced against my abs.

Caspian sat back on his knees and looked over my body. I could see the worry wrapping around his mind. He was conflicted between wanting me and not wanting me to see him.

"If you feel more comfortable, you can leave your shirt on," I said quietly.

Caspian looked up at me and frowned. He bit into the corner of his bottom lip before shaking his head. With his mind made up, he reached for the hem of his shirt and quickly whipped it up over his head. The scars were bad. They wrapped around his throat and ran down over most of his chest and right arm to his stomach and then dipped down into the waistband of his pants. I couldn't imagine the pain he must have been in to go through that.

Caspian didn't lift his head as he breathed out a few heavy breaths. His fear of rejection was so strong. I wish he could see inside me and know that his scars didn't change him. He was still my mate. I wanted him. Mother fate had chosen him for me. That was all that mattered. She didn't make mistakes. He was mine and I was his.

Chapter Six

C aspian

I kept watching Burgess's face for him to recoil in disgust. I was nervous. The only people that had seen the full extent of the damage done to my body were me and the doctors. Not even Macklin knew how far the scars covered my skin. But looking into Burgess's face there was no disgust. I couldn't say if it was who he was or whether it was the heat doing it. I was so uncertain.

Biologically I wanted this man more than my next breath. I believed in fate. I also believed that I was never going to meet my fated mate. Yet Mother fate has a way to do things that I don't understand. Of all the people, it happened to be my best friend's brother and the man that was going to tattoo me to make me feel more attractive. And yet he lay there completely naked looking at me like I was a tall glass of water, and he was dying of thirst.

"Caspian, I'm trying to be a patient man, but I want you to fuck me," Burgess whined, shaking me out of my inner monologue.

His cock was thick, veiny, uncut, and weeping. The red crown looked like it could explode at any moment. The scent of his slick was strong and heady. My cock was aching in the confines of my sweats. I sucked in a deep breath and dropped my pants and boxers in one go.

Burgess moaned as my cock bounced with freedom. He licked his lips and sat up, reaching out his hands, he grasped my hip. My right hip was marred with scars and yet he touched it like he didn't care. The only thing on his mind was my cock. Opening his mouth wide, Burgess swallowed my shaft down to the back of his throat.

The feeling of his tongue as it slid along the base of my cock nearly had my knees buckling beneath me. I thrust my hands through his hair and tipped my head back on my shoulders. My eyes rolled and I let the feeling of pleasure wrap around me. My balls were tight, and I knew that if I didn't get inside Burgess soon, I was going to blow my load down his throat.

I moved my hips and my cock fell from his red, rosy lips with a pop. Burgess looked up at me with those hazel eyes, hooded heavily. His lips glistened with saliva. Gently I pushed on his shoulders, and he laid back on the bed. I lifted his legs and shuffled him to the edge of the bed. Wrapping his ankles around my waist, I bent at the knees and lined the head of my cock up with his entrance, which pulsed with need.

Burgess's eyes were glazed with lust and his breaths were coming out in pants as I ran the head of my cock up and down his crease over his hole.

"Please, Caspian," he moaned. His moans went straight to my dick. Fuck, this man was beautiful.

Slowly as I could I pushed forward until his hole opened and began to swallow the head of my cock, sucking it past that tight ring of muscles. I groaned as I slowly thrust, filling Burgess up until I was bottomed out.

Burgess groaned and wound his hands around my neck. His eyes were firmly on mine as I started to thrust in and out of him. "Yes, just there," Burgess whispered as my cock rocked over his prostate.

I rolled my hips again to hit the same spot and delighted in the way Burgess tilted his head back, exposing his long neck. His hole tightened around my cock, encouraging my knot to form as I continued to move in and out of him. The larger my knot the less movement. My incisors lengthened and I knew that I wasn't going to last much longer. I needed to make this man mine.

"Burgess, please tell me you want to be mine," I said.

Burgess stared into my eye with all seriousness. "Make me yours, Caspian," he said with a husky voice.

My alpha didn't give me any more time to think as it took over. With a roar, I leaned forward and bit into Burgess's skin. At the same time, my body was sent soaring into the heights of pleasure. I heard Burgess cry out and felt the sticky cum hit our stomachs as his answering bite sunk into my chest just above my heart.

I licked over the bite mark on Burgess's chest and looked down at the flesh that was quickly scarring. I looked up into Burgess's eyes who was watching me with a serene smile.

"Did we do the right thing?" I asked.

"I did," he replied with a grin. "I'm not sure you did."

I chuckled. "Oh yeah, I think I did."

Burgess grinned. "So, wanna plan your tattoo while we are stuck?"

I barked out a laugh and nodded my head as I carefully maneuvered us up the bed to lay more comfortably.

Chapter Seven

Burgess

Caspian and I spent the rest of the day and night in bed. We did a lot of fucking, but we also did a lot of talking, getting to know one another. I'd looked closely at his scars and discussed with him what I would be able to do. Unfortunately, that scarring on his face was just still too sensitive to tattoo over, but the rest would be fine. It was likely to hurt more than a normal tattoo, but I assured Caspian we could go as slowly as he liked.

That afternoon I'd worked up a start on a design. Caspian said he wanted to work a phoenix into the design. He wanted something that represented new life. I thought it was fitting, especially now that we were mated and there was going to be a good chance that I would be pregnant.

The morning after meeting Caspian I got out of bed reluctantly and showered, slipping on the clothes I'd worn to his house. I had to open Shifter Ink. I had a few appointments that I was expecting.

"Will you come back tonight?" Caspian asked with a touch of vulnerability in his voice.

I grinned over at my mate and nodded my head. "Yep, I sure will. Oh, and hey I don't want to overwhelm you, but this weekend we are celebrating one of my nephew's birthdays. He is turning seven. All my brothers will be there, along with their mates and children. I'd love it if you came with me so you could meet everyone."

Caspian smiled but I could see the fear in his body language.

"You already know Macklin and Jericho. They are all like that. No one will treat you like anyone other than family. My Mama will tell you that you need to eat more. She will fuss all over us and demand to know when we are giving her grandchildren."

Caspian chuckled and sighed. "Yeah, alright, that would be good."

I smiled and wrapped my arms around his waist, lifting my face to kiss his cheek. "I'll see you tonight when I come back."

Caspian smiled and pressed a firm kiss against my lips, instantly tangling our tongues together. I groaned and ground my hips against his. I could easily shrug off work and go back to bed with my mate, but I had a shop to run. I reluctantly broke the kiss and looked up into Caspian's face.

"I gotta dash, but I will be back here tonight, and we can pick up where we left off," I said pressing another quick peck on his lips.

"Looking forward to it," he replied huskily.

I grinned and turned to leave the house. With a sigh as I climbed into the car, I looked back at the house. We hadn't discussed where we would live. I currently lived above my shop, but it would be good to move away. My little apartment had been handy. But I wanted a family home. Somewhere that our children could run about and play. Caspian's house would be perfect.

I drove to work in a daze. My mind continued to dream of all the things that were to come. Children, I wanted so many of them. I would home school them and teach them about the nature around us. I would teach them their magic. Caspian would teach them skills. I could see our lives together as long and happy.

I opened the shop with my head still in the happy clouds. Switching off the alarm and flicking on the lights, I went through the shop making sure my artists cleaned up their stations before they left work the day before. It was something I harped on about all the time. I demanded cleanliness and hygiene from all my artists. They put up with it and truthfully, I never had anything to complain about. But it didn't mean I was going to be lacking.

"Hey Burgess," Chase called as he came into the shop. I turned and grinned at the vampire. He was well known for his scarification work. When I'd told Caspian about him, he couldn't believe that people would willingly put scars on their bodies.

But like I explained to Caspian, there is a difference between having scarification in patterns that the client wanted, compared to scars caused by an accident like Caspian's. He didn't ask for those scars.

"Woah," Chase said lifting his sunglasses to the top of his head as he skidded to a halt in front of me.

His eyes roved over my body, before settling on the top of the mating mark that was on my chest. It poked just above the V-neck of my t-shirt. I glanced down and chuckled.

"Alright, who is the lucky alpha?" Chase asked.

"His name is Caspian. He is the guy I was telling you about that had been in the fire and wanted tattoos to cover them up."

Chase's eyes widened and his mouth dropped open. "Holy shit, Mother fate has some amazing timing. The way she brought the two of you together is awe-inspiring."

I nodded my head and grinned. "Even with the scars, he is the most beautiful man I've ever met. When he is feeling a bit more confident to leave the house, I'll bring him in to meet you all."

"That would be fantastic. I look forward to meeting him," Chase said as the front door of the shop opened and Sloane came in with the perpetual smile, she always wore.

"Hey guys," she said brightly.

"Hey Sloane, guess what?" Chase said glancing over at me for permission to blurt my news. I grinned and nodded my head.

"What?" she asked standing and cocking her head to the side.

"Burgess is now a mated man."

Sloane's eyes widened and a slow grin filled out over her face. "Burgess that is fucking awesome," she squealed. She stepped into my arms and pulled me into a tight bear hug. "I can't wait to meet them."

"You will, soon hopefully. His name is Caspian."

"Oh, the guy you were meeting yesterday?"

I nodded my head and smiled. "It was fate."

"Yeah, it sure was."

Chapter Eight

C aspian

I was sitting on my couch with a goofy smile on my face. I couldn't believe this was my life. I had a mate. A motherfucking mate. I couldn't believe it. If my scars would have allowed it, I would have burst into a massive belly laugh. I was beyond grateful that Mother fate even saw fit to give me a mate. Let alone one that was as beautiful as Burgess.

My phone buzzed on the coffee table and when I looked down at the ID, I saw that it was Macklin calling. I wasn't sure whether Burgess had told him about the latest events in our life.

"Hey man," I said as I answered, it was impossible to keep the joy out of my voice.

"So, the tattoo planning went well?" Macklin asked.

I chuckled. "Um. Yeah," I replied. "Have you spoken to Burgess?"

"No? Should I?"

I hummed. I wasn't sure if Burgess would want me to tell his brother, but I also knew that there was going to be no keeping a secret from Macklin. The man was a lie detector. It came from all his training.

"Well, I've got some news, and please promise me you aren't going to come and punch me in the face," I started.

Macklin growled in his throat. "Did you hurt my brother?"

"No, shit, no nothing like that," I said quickly. "We are mates."

Silence greeted me on the phone. I glanced at the screen to make sure that Macklin hadn't ended the call.

He cleared his throat. "Well, that's alright then. I don't really know what to say. I'm jealous as hell that you got a mate. I'm deliriously happy because that makes you more than my best mate, it makes you a brother. But I'm also slightly perturbed because it's my brother that is your mate."

I chuckled. "I will take the deliriously happy emotion please."

Macklin laughed and sighed. "I am happy for you man. Just don't hurt him. Burgess is tender-hearted. He feels things so much more than we all do. He mothers all of us, sometimes worse than Mama does."

"I have no intentions of hurting him. We did a lot of talking yesterday and last night. I was more open with him than I had been with anyone, I think ever."

I could hear the smile in Macklin's voice when he spoke again. "I'm glad, man. You deserve that happiness. Burgess is a great omega. He will make you happy if you let him."

"I will let him," I replied.

We chatted about the tattoo design that Burgess had come up with before I promised to catch up with Macklin on the weekend for his nephew's birthday. I sat back on the couch and sighed. Macklin's words played over in my mind. I didn't want to hurt Burgess. That was the last thing I wanted to do.

The truth was, I didn't know how to be in a relationship. I mean I guess no one ever really does. But for me, I never had parents that showed me. I was born to a pair of fae. Some foster parents told me they'd been killed, others told me that I'd been taken away by the government. I didn't know the truth. Nor had I ever bothered to try to find out. I just wasn't interested.

I grew up in a series of foster homes of humans. In some homes, I was taught that I was evil because I was fae. In others, I became a spectacle. And then other homes just didn't really care. One thing I was always grateful for, was that I was good at school. I always got good grades, and the homes that I was sent to were all in Lalbert, which meant I didn't have to change schools.

I was able to get into university easily and then when I joined Lalbert Fire, it made it possible to buy my home. It never bothered me not to have a family. Not until the accident. When I first came home from the hospital, I had longed to have brothers, sisters, or parents that would help me. When I was in pain at night, it would have been nice to have someone hold my hand and tell me it was going to be alright.

Those mornings when I was vomiting with grief because I couldn't look in the mirror, or I couldn't even face going outside, would have been so much easier with someone by my side. But there wasn't anyone I could call on. I mean I could have asked Macklin once I met him, I knew that he would drop everything to come and help me. But that wasn't what I needed. I needed someone that understood me.

And then Mother fate brought me, Burgess. I knew that my future was going to be very different. I was about to become stronger. I knew I could because I had my mate by my side.

Chapter Nine

B urgess
I had about half an hour between clients so knew that it was the best time to give Mama a ring and let her know that she could expect another person on the weekend.

"Burgess my love," she answered making me chuckle. One thing Mama never did was make any of us feel like a burden for ringing her. She always sounded excited to hear from us.

"Hey, Mama. I've got some news," I said.

"Oh really? Tell me." From the sound of her voice, I had the distinct feeling she already knew what was about to come. I mean it was pretty much the only thing I'd be ringing with news for. Any other time I just rang her for a chat.

"I met my mate," I said with a grin on my face.

Mama squealed into the phone. "I'm thrilled," she cried. "All my babies are finding their mates. Tell me about them?"

"His name is Caspian. He is a fae. He used to be a firefighter until an accident. I met him through Macklin."

"Oh, I remember that accident, Jericho told me about it. It was awful. I tried to get Jericho to invite him over, but he never answered any of Jericho's calls. I figured he just needed time. I think I've heard Macklin talk about him too. So, are we going to be meeting him on the weekend?"

"Yes," I said. "He agreed to come and meet you all. I imagine he is going to be nervous. He is still very self-conscious about his scarring. I tried to explain to him that none of you would care about it."

"That's right. The physical means nothing. It's all about the person beneath the skin."

"I'm happy that it is us that he is joining. I know that with your love and my brothers will all make him feel like he is part of the family."

"They sure will. You know that anyone is welcome in our family and if they are fated to one of you boys, they are even more welcomed."

"Thank you, Mama. I love you."

"Oh, sweet boy. I love you too. I always have and I always will. I can't wait to meet Caspian. Does he have a favorite food?"

I chuckled. "I told him that you would want to know. And yes, he said he loves anything with pumpkin."

"Excellent, I'll make my pumpkin salad, especially for him. I might even make a pumpkin gratin, I remember that March loved that too."

"That would be fantastic, thank you, Mama."

"Anytime baby boy. I'll let you get back to work. I'm gonna go tell everyone that another of my babies has met his mate."

I laughed as I said goodbye to my Mama. She reacted the same way every time one of us boys found our mates. Even when Bacchus found Anghus. They were both alphas and weren't sure if an omega would be fated to them. But that didn't matter to Mama, she was even prepared to surrogate a child for them if they wanted it. It wouldn't matter who we brought home, if they were fated to us, then they instantly became part of the family.

Hell, even when we were growing up and brought friends home, it didn't matter what they looked like, it didn't matter if they were supernatural's or humans. They were welcomed into the home as one of the family.

I wasn't sure how Jericho would react about Caspian and pondered whether I should perhaps give him a call to give him the heads up. I had a feeling that Macklin would ring Caspian seeing as they were best friends. Macklin would want to know how the tattoo planning went. I wasn't too worried about Macklin's opinion. Although he struggled badly with PTSD, he was still easygoing. He was protective of all his brothers, but he truly believed in fate.

The front door of the shop opened, and I looked up to see the devil himself walking into the shop. "Macklin," I said with a laugh. "I was just thinking about you."

Macklin grinned. "Me or maybe another man, my best friend perhaps?"

I barked out a laugh. "So, you've spoken to Caspian then?"

Macklin nodded his head and sat in the seat beside me. "Yeah, I did. I'm happy for you. Just be patient with him. It's going to be challenging. He doesn't like to admit it, but the accident fucked with his head."

I nodded. "Yeah, I can imagine. I saw the covers over all the mirrors. I didn't say anything about them. I don't want to push him too fast."

Macklin smiled. "It might be worth coming along to the group with us. I mean ask Caspian first, he might not want you there, but it will help you get a bit of an understanding."

"I'll talk to Caspian. I don't want to be a pushy bitch either. I don't want him to feel like now that we are mated, I'm going to try to take over his life and push him to do things he's not comfortable with."

Macklin smiled and held out his arms, pulling me into a tight hug. "I can't think of a better guy for him to be mated with. You just keep being you and I know that he will open up."

"Thank you," I said with a little sob. Macklin didn't talk a lot. He tended to keep quiet because he thought he was a burden. But I missed my little brother. We were so close growing up. He was wildly protective of me. We were the closest in age. There were only six months between the two of us. We'd been more like twins than individual brothers.

"I love you, man," Macklin said as he kissed me on top of the head and let me go.

"I love you too," I replied with tears in my eyes. I waved my hand over my face and blinked wildly. "You're going to make me cry."

Macklin chuckled. "Don't do that, you'll ruin your makeup." I barked out a laugh and shook my head. "When is your next appointment?"

I glanced at my watch. "In about ten minutes."

Macklin smiled and nodded. "Will you book me in for some work? I've got a bit of an idea."

"Of course, you know I love tattooing my brothers."

"Yeah, but Obsidian and Bacchus are the only ones that ever take you up on it."

"Only cause Asher is scared of pain, he only likes to doll it out, not receiving it. And Jericho is too fussy to decide what he wants. Drake is never home long enough to get work done."

Macklin chuckled and nodded his head. "Mama said that Drake was coming home for an extended time. He is talking about setting up his own salon here in Lalbert."

My eyes widened. Our brother Drake was a hairstylist and makeup artist. He often worked overseas with celebrities. His work on movies was renowned. It was rare that he was home for very long. I missed seeing him. It would be great to see him.

"Yeah? What's bringing him home?" I asked.

Macklin shrugged his shoulders. "I don't know. Mama thinks something happened. But he hasn't said anything. You know Drake, he never says anything until he is well and truly ready."

I sighed and nodded. Drake had always worried Mama and Dad. It wasn't that he was secretive he just kept things to himself. He was fiercely independent and didn't like to ask for help. Not until it was at a point where he just physically couldn't do it by himself. It meant that the problems he finally brought to the family were huge. For him to be coming back to Lalbert for an extended amount of time had to mean something was wrong.

I guess time would tell. I worried about all my brothers. Well, not Asher or Bacchus so much now that they were mated. But the others I still did.

Chapter Ten

C aspian
"Hi, honey I'm home," Burgess called with laughter, as he came in through the front door just before six that night.

I might have admitted that I was waiting on tenterhooks, wondering if he would come back to my house. Part of me thought he might change his mind during the day, and I'd never see him again. But when I heard his car pull into my driveway butterflies took flight in my belly with excitement.

"Hey," I chuckled as I stood from the couch and walked to greet Burgess with a kiss.

"Mmm, a man could get used to coming home to that," he chuckled.

I grinned. "Everyday."

Burgess looked up into my eyes and smiled broadly. "Yeah, every day. Sorry, I'm a bit later, I didn't want to be presumptuous, but I wanted to bring back some clothes. My staff isn't going to want to see me wearing the same clothes every day."

I shook my head as I realized that was something we hadn't talked about. "Of course. Shit, we never even discussed living arrangements."

Burgess waved his hand and dropped his bag onto the floor beside the living room door before taking my hand in his and leading me over to the couch. In society, alpha's were typically the leaders. It wasn't a conscious thing; it just was how it ended up being. Yet in my brief relationship with Burgess, I felt like he was the alpha, and I was the omega. I wondered if I should feel weird about it, but I didn't. In fact, I liked having someone taking over and dealing with the stuff that I forgot.

"I currently live above my shop. If you would like me to, of course, I could move in with you. I mean if you would rather have your privacy, that I understand too, I can stay living above the shop," he said.

I frowned and shook my head. "No. I want you to live with me."

Burgess smiled. "Well, that was easy," he laughed. "I'll organize my brothers to help me move my personal belongings over."

"Sure, and if you need me to move any of the furniture or you want to get rid of everything just say the word."

Burgess shook his head. "Na, I don't own any special furniture. I like what you've got here. I love the feel of it. It's more just my clothes, a few knick-knacks, pictures, and my art supplies."

"Oh, this place has four bedrooms. We could turn one of them into an art space for you," I said as I jumped off the couch and pulled Burgess up to follow me.

He followed behind me as I raced down the hallway. We had barely left the bedroom the day and night before, so I hadn't had a chance to give him a tour of the house. "There are three bedrooms on this side and then our bedroom on the other side of the house."

"Well, that will come in handy when we have children, they won't hear our night romps," Burgess chuckled.

I stopped in the center of the hallway and turned around with my eye wide. "Children? Holy shit, I didn't even think of children. You might be pregnant?"

Burgess nodded his head. "I could be. I guess we won't know for a few more days yet, but if the creator sees fit, I will be pregnant. Did you want children? Probably should have checked that before we got busy yesterday."

I snorted and nodded my head. "Yeah, I want kids. I've always liked the idea of having children. Not that I'm sure I'd make a very good dad."

Burgess pulled me into his arms and pressed a kiss to my lips. "I think you will make a fine father. The only thing you must do to get it right is love them and protect them. I know that you can do that."

A slow smile formed on my lips, and I nodded. "Yeah, I can do that. Especially if they look like you."

Burgess grinned. "Show me the rooms."

I nodded and turned my attention back to the bedrooms that never got used. They had sat empty, not even with furniture in them. I swung the door to the first room open and Burgess peered inside.

"Wow, they are an empty canvas. The rooms are all this big?"

I nodded my head. "That's what I wanted when I built it. I'd been thinking about one day how I would have a family, and this would be perfect."

Burgess grinned and nodded. "It sure will be. I can already envision it."

I wrapped my arm around Burgess's shoulder and glanced around the room. The image was easy to imagine. Beautiful ginger children running around, laughing, and playing. Toys scattered everywhere. I'd even create a special place in the garden so that they could grow whatever they wanted. A swing in one of the big oak trees out the back, or maybe a cubby house. The more I thought about it, the more it filled me with excitement. The creator truly was looking out for me.

Chapter Eleven

B urgess

"I'm a bit nervous," Caspian admitted to me as we pulled up to my family home. I killed the engine and turned in my seat.

"You already know that Macklin will be there, and I know it's been a long time since you've seen Jericho, but he hasn't changed since you knew him. My family will accept you. But if you want to leave at any time, just say the word, and I will pack everything up and we will leave. I just want you to try to say hello at the very least," I said.

We'd talked a lot over the week, and I knew that he was nervous about seeing Jericho again. He'd admitted that he'd pushed everyone away after the accident. Even with me assuring him that Jericho wasn't mad, he was still frightened to see him. I understood it. Caspian had shut himself off completely after the accident. He pushed everyone close to him away. Everyone except Macklin and that was only because Macklin was in the unique position of understanding what Caspian was going through.

Caspian took a deep breath. I knew that Mama would be watching through the window, but she also knew that she couldn't overwhelm Caspian. Both Macklin and I had explained to her what we knew about Caspian's case.

The front door to the house opened and Macklin came out onto the porch. I could see that he was trying to decide whether to come down and interrupt or not. I gave him a smile and nodded my head which was enough to prompt Macklin in approaching the car. He opened the passenger door and looked down at Caspian.

"How are you feeling man?" Macklin asked.

"Fucking terrified. My butthole is puckering," Caspian said trying to make a joke.

"I know that feeling. Fuck, the first time I came home after being in the hospital for so long, I was terrified."

Caspian looked up at Macklin with a small frown. "But they are your family."

Macklin nodded. "Yeah, but I wasn't the same son or brother they sent to war. I was having massive nightmares, I was jaded and angry."

Caspian did have nightmares. There had been a couple of nights during the week that I'd woken to him screaming. It sounded like he was reliving the accident in his dreams. It hurt to know it was happening, especially considering there was nothing I could do to ease it. I had just held him until he settled and fell back asleep. The next morning it was like he didn't remember the dream, he never mentioned it and I didn't know how to bring it up without him worrying.

I worked out very quickly that Caspian worried about a lot of things but being a burden to someone was his biggest concern. I just had to keep reassuring him that he wasn't a burden to me. Mother's fate wouldn't have brought us together just to burden me. That's not how she worked. But it was going to take a lot of time before that sunk into his head.

"I promise that my family is really easy going," Macklin said. "Between me and Burgess, I promise you will be alright. The kids will probably stare at first, but that's because they are kids."

I appreciated the way that Macklin didn't pull punches, he prepared his friend for what he could expect with complete honesty. It was a great attribute, and I could see Caspian start to relax. He took a deep breath and nodded his head before unbuckling his seat belt. I grinned up at my brother and he winked his good eye at me.

Stepping out of the car, I walked ahead of Macklin and Caspian who were still talking quietly behind me. Macklin was encouraging Caspian. It made me love my brother even more. He was so patient with Caspian, and I could see just how deeply he cared about his friend.

When I swung the door open Mama was standing in the living room waiting for us. I smirked knowing that she had been looking through the window at us. Mama scrunched her nose at me, causing me to chuckle.

"Mama, this is my mate. Caspian. This is my Mama, Abigail," I introduced.

Mama stepped towards Caspian and looked up at him with a wide smile on her face. "Hello, Caspian. I'm so glad to have you as part of the family," she said before taking him into her arms in a tight hug. It was how my Mama greeted everyone.

"Thank you," Caspian said with a smile before hugging her back. I watched as his body relaxed and he started to realize that it wasn't as scary as he'd built up in his head.

"Now, you take as long as you need to, but when you are ready, why don't you come on out and meet everyone else," Mama said.

Caspian bit into his bottom lip before quickly glancing between me and Macklin. "I'd like that," he replied.

I reached out and took Caspian's hand in mine and slowly we walked towards the back door where I knew everyone would be in the garden. I was so proud of my mate. He was way out of his comfort zone, but he was doing it.

Chapter Twelve

Caspian

My stomach had been full of rampaging elephants. My hands trembled and I could have happily made Burgess turn the car around and take me home. I knew that Burgess's family would be welcoming. Macklin was my best friend. I'd been friends with Jericho before the accident and Burgess was my mate. I knew that they weren't the sort to judge. But it didn't stop my panic.

What I never expected was Abigail to embrace me, like I was just part of the family. She didn't look at me with pity. She didn't reel back with disgust. She just simply accepted me, scars, and all. That I wasn't prepared for.

I took a deep breath and looked between Macklin and Burgess. "Okay, I'm alright, I think."

Macklin grinned at me and slapped my back. "Believe me the rest of the family is just the same as Mama."

I smiled and nodded my head. Burgess gave my hand a squeeze and when I looked at him, he smiled and winked. "Remember what I said, if it gets too much, just say the word and we will leave."

I leaned over and pressed a kiss on Burgess's cheek. "Thank you, baby."

"Alright, enough of that," Macklin groaned causing me to chuckle.

"Let's go meet your family then. I owe Jericho an apology."

Macklin smiled and led the way to the back of the house. The house was a typical family home. There were pictures of all the Rigby brothers as well as the grandchildren. I could tell that there was a lot of love and laughter in this house. It had that feel about it. Abigail's personality seemed to pour out into every room.

As we exited the back door, I could hear men chatting along with children laughing and playing. Macklin walked into the backyard first, followed by Burgess and me.

"Uncle Burgie," a little voice called out.

"Bear, Iver, McKenna, and Ivy babes," Burgess said as three children ran towards him. The youngest was a little girl who was being held by a man I assumed was her father. Burgess kneeled in front of them and opened his arms to hug them all.

A little boy that appeared to be around seven looked up at me, his eyes seemed to bore straight into my soul. "You are going to be a really good father and teach your son everything," he said.

My mouth dropped open. It wasn't at all what I had expected to come out of his mouth.

"Iver, what have we talked about just blurting out everything you read?" A huge man with long dark hair and a long beard said.

Iver turned to who I assumed was his father with a roll of his eyes. "I have to, or it bubbles up inside me and I can't keep it in."

I lowered myself so that I was at Iver's level and stuck my hand out to shake his. "Thank you for your words, Iver. I appreciate hearing them. I've been feeling very worried about what I would be like as a Dad, so your words mean a lot."

Iver grinned and nodded his head. "I just say what the creator tells me."

I frowned. Burgess had told me that his family was very powerful. They were very proud shifters and supernaturals who believed a lot in the creator and the power that was bestowed on all supernaturals. It wasn't something that I'd ever really learned about. Having grown up with humans, I didn't know a lot about the supernatural world. I certainly didn't know what it meant to be fae.

Iver leaned in towards me. "You are going to be a Dad to a little boy. He wants to be named Thatcher. He will be fae, but he will also have the power of a lion shifter. He will be very strong. Like Bear," he whispered with a quick glance over his shoulder towards his father who was watching him with a raised brow.

Iver ducked his head and giggled before he ran off towards where the other children were now playing. I stood just as Iver's father came towards me with his hand out to shake.

"Hi, Caspian. I'm Anghus. I apologize for my son's constant need to tell everyone everything. You'll learn very quickly there are no surprises when he is around."

I chuckled and shook my head. "So, he really could see the child he was talking about?"

Anghus nodded his head. "Yep. He has correctly predicted everyone. Part of his powers is that he can connect directly to the creator and to the unborn children."

I looked over at Burgess who was hugging his brothers. "So, that means Burgess is pregnant?"

Anghus grinned and winked. "I'd say it might be time to do a pregnancy test." My mouth dropped open. I was excited but terrified all in the same breath. "Come on, let me introduce you to the other members of the family.

Anghus guided me over to where another man who I knew had to be one of the Rigby brothers stood with a smaller man. "These are my mates, Bacchus, who is Burgess's younger brother, and Joachim."

I glanced between the three men. "You have two mates?"

Anghus smiled and nodded. "You didn't grow up around supernaturals?" I shook my head and felt my cheeks blush. "No shame in it. I'm a gargoyle, Bacchus is a kraken and Joachim is a griffin. We are all mystical's which means that we are often fated to more than one mate."

I hummed and frowned. "What does that mean for me? I'm fae."

"You could have another mate out there, but I get the feeling that Burgess is your one," Joachim answered.

I smiled and nodded. "I think I would rather that."

"The creator will never give you more than you could handle," Anghus replied.

Chapter Thirteen

B urgess
I could feel Caspian's nerves as Jericho approached him. I took hold of Caspian's hand to reassure him that Jericho didn't have any bad feelings. I'd rang Jericho during the week and told him about Caspian. Jericho told me that he was looking forward to seeing Caspian again.

"Casp," Jericho said with an easy smile. Out of all of us brothers, Jericho had always been the most serious. He didn't do a lot of talking, he never really did. The youngest of all the Rigby brothers he was often hard to get to know. He kept everything inside and didn't let much out.

"Jericho," Caspian breathed. "I owe you an apology."

Jericho frowned and shook his head but stopped when Caspian held his hand up.

"I do. I turned my back on everyone. I should have answered your calls or at the very least texted you back. I was an ass for not doing that at the very least."

"Caspian, every one of us understood. What you went through was fucked. We knew that you were in a dark place. But we understood that you didn't want to reach out to us."

Caspian sighed and nodded. "I shouldn't have been that way. I recognize that all of you were trying to help, and it was me that pushed you all away."

Jericho shook his head. "You didn't push us away. You just put a boundary in place, we were all prepared to wait for you to be ready."

Caspian frowned. "Really?"

Jericho smiled. "Really. We just wanted you to be ready, but we were all prepared to wait for you to be ready to talk to us again."

"Thank you," Caspian said with a smile.

Jericho grinned and reached out pulling his friend into a hug. "Whenever you are ready and want to, why don't you come into the firehouse and say hello. I promise that everyone misses you. We still talk about you regularly. The place isn't the same without your laughter."

It was interesting to hear Jericho talk about Caspian as being full of laughter. He wasn't like that at all anymore. I guess the accident didn't just steal his unflawed face and body, but it stole his joy and a lot of his personality.

Caspian nodded and bit into his lip. "I will try to get there. I want to start pushing myself to get out there. I can't hide forever."

Jericho's smile was broad. "It would be great to see you. But only when you are ready man, no rush," he said as he patted Caspian's shoulder. "Hey, do you remember all the practical jokes you used to play on us?"

Caspian chuckled and nodded his head. "I never knew how you guys didn't catch on."

Jericho threw his head back and laughed. "Nothing was as funny as cap taking his helmet off and having a black rim across his forehead. He had no idea and was getting so angry at everyone laughing at him."

Caspian laughed. "I nearly lost my job for that one. He had a press conference to give that afternoon and couldn't get the marker off his head. He had to go on national television with a black stripe across his forehead. All the reporters were more interested in what the hell was on his head than what he was there to speak about."

Jericho threw his head back and laughed out a huge belly laugh as he nodded. "Oh fuck, I forgot about that part. How did you manage to keep your job?"

"I had to clean the entire quarters. He even made me scrub the kitchen tiles with a fucking toothbrush."

I couldn't stop the goofy smile that sat on my lips as I listened to Jericho and Caspian catching up. It was so hard to imagine Caspian being the joker that Jericho said he was. I hoped that one day I would get a glimpse into that person. While Jericho and Caspian talked, I left them and walked over to greet my other brothers.

"Burgess," Obsidian said as he pulled me into a tight hug.

"Sid, how's business?" I asked.

Obsidian grinned. "Really good. We've been flat out thanks to Anghus and all the Devil's Advocates. I've already had to hire on three more mechanics and two people to work the office."

"That's amazing," I said. "You'll be rolling in it."

Obsidian chuckled. "It will all go into a house I'm planning on building. I bought the land the other week, just waiting for a settlement, and then I'll start building. It's a huge piece of property, I was thinking of putting a workshop out there and starting to build custom bikes. Donte is really into the bikes as is Walker."

Donte was March's brother-in-law, while Walker was a young guy that Obsidian had met through the Devil's Advocates. His adopted parents were Pax and Holland. Pax worked for the AJE Authority with Bacchus. As soon as Walker had met Anghus and the other Devil's Advocates he found his home. Obsidian hired him on as an apprentice mechanic and as they say, the rest is history.

"Where is the property?" I asked.

"Just on the outskirts of Lalbert, just off Knox Road."

"Oh awesome, that's just around the corner from Caspian's house."

Obsidian grinned. "So, how is being mated?"

"So far I'm loving every minute."

"Have you done a pregnancy test yet?"

I laughed and shook my head. "No, but I'm not sure I even need to with Iver around," I said as I remembered the words of my nephew about the boy that was growing inside me.

"He definitely has a gift," Obsidian laughed. "But do a test anyway."

Chapter Fourteen

C aspian

The day with Burgess's family was so good. I was surprised by how welcoming they had been and how relaxed I felt. Even the kids had warmed up to me at once. I noticed that Iver was the leader of the motley crew. Once he was chatting to me about being a firefighter then the rest of the kids followed.

Bear was a handful for his poor parents. The little boy preferred to be in his shifted state of a bear than human, it was hilarious to watch Asher, who I found out owned the kink club in town and was a Dom, try to reign in his headstrong son.

Burgess was driving back to my house, and I had a small smile on my lips as I replayed the day. Jericho and I caught up about everyone at the firehouse. I was very tempted to make a visit, but I wasn't sure if I could do it. I'd purposely pushed all of them away after the accident. I was too afraid to see any of them again.

"Did you have fun today?" Burgess asked, breaking into my inner thoughts.

I looked over at my mate and smiled. "I did. Your family is fantastic. I should've already known that, seeing as you and Macklin are awesome."

Burgess grinned. "Well, I mean, I'm the best out of all of them."

I barked out a laugh and nodded my head. "You sure are baby, you sure are."

Burgess's grin turned salacious as he side-eyed me. "I'm the sexiest too."

I growled possessively and reached my hand over the center console to stroke between Burgess's thighs up to his cock that was already halfway to being hard.

"You sure are," I replied as I fumbled to undo the button and fly.

Snaking my fingers into the waistband of his boxers I slipped Burgess's cock from the confines. The shaft was hard, and the head was already leaking pre-cum. Burgess moaned but when I glanced at his face, I noticed a small frown as he fought to concentrate on the road. It was dangerous but I couldn't bring myself to stop.

Slowly I stroked up and down his shaft, enjoying every hitch in his breath. I ran my thumb along the underside of the head and Burgess let out a long moan.

"Fuck that is good," he groaned.

I chuckled and continued to stroke up and down. My own cock was throbbing in my pants. With my other hand, I pulled open my jeans and released my cock from my boxers, and slid my hand in time with my movements on Burgess's dick.

"I've got to pull over," Burgess moaned as he slid into a side road that was surrounded by trees. We weren't hidden by any sense of the word but at least we weren't at threat of crashing the car either.

I removed my hand from Burgess's cock, "lean the chair back," I said.

Burgess laid the chair back, to make more room for my shoulders as I leaned over the center console and opened my lips wide. I sucked his dick to the back of my throat, the taste of his pre-cum delighted my taste buds, along with the sounds of his moans in my ears. Bobbing my head up and down I flicked my tongue over the head of his dick. Burgess threaded his hands through my hair and guided my head up and down. His breathing was coming out in deep pants as he thrust his hips, pushing his cock deeper into my throat.

I stroked my hand up and down my own cock, feeling my balls tighten with the threat of orgasm. Burgess cried out, just as my pleasure rocketed over the edge. Jets of hot cum sprayed against my tongue as I sucked everything, he gave me, swallowing him like it was the most delicious meal I'd ever received.

I let go of Burgess's softening cock and sat back in my seat with a small smile playing on my lips.

"Damn you're good at that," Burgess said.

"Plenty of practice," I chuckled.

Burgess growled. "I don't want to hear about others."

I laughed and shook my head. "Baby, you misunderstand. The practice was on me."

When I looked over at Burgess, he was looking at me with wide eyes. He blinked slowly and opened and closed his mouth.

"How?" he finally managed.

I laughed again. "I was a lot younger and a hell of a lot more flexible."

"You're serious? You could suck your own dick?"

I nodded, the look on his face was comical. It was true. My first ever blow job came from myself after stumbling across a short video of a guy doing the same.

"Jesus, that's hot," Burgess said, making me laugh even harder.

Chapter Fifteen

Burgess

The days fell into such a comfortable pace. I found myself falling in love with Caspian a little more every day that passed. He taught me everything about how he'd made his house a place of self-sufficiency. I'd even seen him smiling more often. He would respond to Jericho's texts, and I noticed that he talked more about the guys from the firehouse. He'd even mentioned perhaps going to see them.

He still didn't leave the house very often, except for on Tuesdays when he would catch an uber into his therapy session. In truth, I think the only reason he did was that it was his chance to catch up with Macklin. They were more like brothers than just friends. Their relationship was so strong. It made me happy, not just for Caspian but for Macklin too. He even seemed to become more alive.

"So, Mr. Rigby," Sahara said as she slid into the seat beside me in my station.

I chuckled. "Yes, Sahara."

"Well, we couldn't help but notice that you are starting to develop a little pudge around the middle. And we know that the Rigby's can eat, but we don't think that is the case here."

I rubbed my hand over my belly. A pregnancy test had been on the to-do list for a while, but it was one of those things, I kept meaning to get around to, but didn't. I think it was because I trusted Iver's word and knew that I was pregnant.

"Are you suggesting that I might be pregnant?" I said with a laugh.

Sahara shrugged her shoulders. "Well look, I'm not one to assume or gossip."

I barked out a laugh. Sahara was most definitely one to gossip. That little witch loved nothing more than gossiping. She grinned at me and waved her hand, before reaching into her bag that I hadn't noticed she had on her lap.

"We may have decided that you need to take a pregnancy test," Sahara said pulling out a box.

I grinned and shook my head. "What if I already took one?"

Sahara's eyes widened and a grin formed on her lips. "Did you?"

I laughed again as I shook my head. "No. But thank you. I will go and take one."

"Now?"

"Yes now, Miss bossy pants."

I took the box from Sahara's hands and took it with me into the bathroom. I'd never taken a pregnancy test, but I still knew how they worked. I was with March when he took his test when he discovered he was pregnant with Ivy.

Unpackaging the test, I dropped my pants and pulled out the little cup to pee in. Thinking about anything other than the need to pee, a trickle finally started and once the cup was full, I flushed the toilet and set the cup on the edge of the basin before washing my hands. I dipped the test in the urine and then waited.

It was the longest two minutes of my life. But sure, like eggs, two pink lines were forming. I was pregnant. I grinned and chuckled. Just like Iver predicted. I rubbed my hand down over my little pouch. Sahara was right, I was starting to protrude quite the belly.

"Welcome to the world little man," I whispered as I emptied the cup of urine in the toilet and cleaned up. Washing my hands once more, I swooped up the pregnancy test and went out into the shop.

All my employees were standing waiting. They all wore equal grins, making me laugh. I held the pregnancy test up and crowed. "I'm pregnant."

The shop let out a loud cheer. Orion and Chase crowded me giving me a hug, followed by the others.

"Congratulations, you are going to make the best Papa," Sloane said with a bright smile.

"Thank you. I can't wait to tell Caspian."

"Tell me what?" Caspian asked as he walked in through the front door.

I gasped and glanced up. This was huge. This was the first time that he'd ever come into the shop.

"Caspian," I said with a bright smile before pushing through the group of people that surrounded me and went to him, pressing a kiss to his lips.

"Hey baby," he said with a small chuckle.

"You're here."

Caspian nodded his head and sucked in a deep breath. "I thought it was time."

"I'm so happy. I have something to show you," I said as I lifted the pregnancy test for him to see.

Caspian took it in his hand and looked at the test with scrutiny before looking up into my face. "Is this correct? You're pregnant?"

I chuckled and nodded my head. "We are going to have a baby."

Caspian wrapped his arms around me and kissed me firmly and passionately. A throat cleared behind us and when I looked over Caspian's shoulder, I saw Macklin standing with a small smile on his lips.

Caspian turned and faced my brother. "You're going to be an uncle again."

Macklin grinned and wrapped his arms around the both of us. "That's what all that shouting was about."

I turned back to my employees who were watching with knowing smiles on their faces. "Everyone, this is my mate. Caspian."

Everyone chorused a hello and Caspian raised his hand in a small wave. "I am pleased to meet you all," he said before clearing his throat. "Um, so I'm your one o'clock appointment."

I chuckled. "Casper?"

Caspian grinned as he nodded his head.

"You could have just told me."

Caspian chuckled and shrugged his shoulders. "I wanted to surprise you. But then you surprised me."

I laughed and directed my mate over to my station. We'd been over his tattoo and refined it. I was under the impression that I was going to do it while we were at home, but this was a surprise. He was feeling comfortable enough to come into the shop.

Chapter Sixteen

Caspian

Nobody was going to be able to steal the sheer delirious joy I felt today. Not only had I managed to achieve my goal of going to see Burgess at work, but I discovered I was going to be a father. There wasn't anything better. Burgess and I had spent weeks planning the tattoo that would work best for me.

The design he'd come up with was phenomenal. It was a phoenix bursting from the scars. Although I would be forever scarred, there was no reason it couldn't be beautiful. There wasn't a lot we could do about the scarring on my face. But at that moment it didn't matter. The head of the phoenix would reach just below my chin and the flames would wrap around my neck.

"We will start with some of the outlines today, but I'm going to warn you, that tattooing over scars will hurt more than just an everyday tattoo," Burgess warned. He'd told me this several times during the planning stages.

"It's alright baby. If it gets too much, I'll let you know," I reassured him.

Nothing could hurt as bad as the first pain that I'd felt. Knowing it was my mate that was giving me my tattoo would make the pain worth it. I lay on the bed on my stomach. We were going to start on my back first as the scarring wasn't as bad there.

The shop was buzzing with the sounds of tattoos and chatter as other artists started working on their clients. Macklin had organized to get some work off one of the other artists, Orion. He had a couple of tattoos but nothing big. He was planning to get a big back piece done, a family tree. The branches were twisted with the names of all his family. I loved the idea. It made me start to think about something I could get that would be my little family.

I couldn't wait to meet our little man. I believed Iver was right when he said that we were having a son and that the son would be called Thatcher.

"Alright babe, I'm going to start now, you ready?" Burgess said breaking into my thoughts.

"I'm all good," I replied.

The buzz of his tattoo gun started, and I felt him lean over my back, his gloved hands pressed on the skin of my lower back. The first swipe of the tattoo gun took my breath away. It wasn't so much that it hurt, it was just such an unusual sensation. It was like being bitten by a mosquito over and over.

"You alright?" Burgess asked after he did that first line.

"Yep, just wasn't prepared for what it would feel like," I replied.

Burgess chuckled. "Yeah, it always takes everyone by surprise. Not too much pain?"

"No, the pain is fine."

"Good, I'll keep going. Try not to move and just let me know if you need a break."

"I will, baby," I assured him as I reached out and gave his knee a squeeze.

"And don't feel up the artist or you might get more than you bargain for."

I laughed and squeezed Burgess's thigh again. He leaned forward and pressed a quick kiss to my cheek before he started the gun again and began to tattoo. It didn't take long before the feeling of the needles became a background sensation. Every now and then he would hit a sensitive spot, but for the most part, it was easy going. We hadn't started in the worst of the scarring, which I had expected would be more painful.

I didn't know how long I'd been laying on my belly, drifting in and out of sleep when the gun eased, and Burgess wiped down over my back. He leaned back in his seat and stretched his arms above his head.

"That's the outline for your back done. I'll leave it like that for today, I don't want to try and do too much. The skin will be sensitive even with your elevated healing. So, we will start on your chest next time," he said. "Carefully stand and check it out in the mirror and then I'll wrap it up for you."

I stood feeling my head spin a little from lying down for so long. I glanced around the room and noticed that Orion was just wrapping Macklin up. Another man was sitting at a station having bits of flesh cut out of his leg. My eyes widened and my mouth dropped open as I took in what he was getting done. In another station, a girl was piercing a man's nipples.

I walked over to the mirror and turned to look. My eyes widened. Even though we'd just gotten through the outline it was perfect. Burgess had created the start of the scene. The flames of the phoenix worked around my scars. The raised scars would become the flames on my back. Tears prickled at my eye as I took it in. I could almost envision it when it was finished.

"I love it," I said quietly. When I looked back at Burgess, he was watching me with a small smile on his lips.

"I'm glad."

"Baby, you are so talented," I gushed as I looked back into the mirror.

"Isn't he?" Macklin said as he approached me. "I love it. I can see it coming alive already."

I nodded my head and looked back at my mate who was beaming with pride. Damn, I got lucky.

Chapter Seventeen

Burgess

I couldn't be more excited to be sitting in a doctor's office. Caspian was sitting beside me and although he was jittery and wore a cap pulled down tight on his head, I was still so proud that he'd come along. He said there was nothing that was going to stop him from coming to see our little one in the ultrasound.

"Burgess," Reagan called. I'd met her several times through helping out with friends who found themselves, single parents, as well as joining Joachim and March once each.

Reagan grinned as Caspian, and I walked towards her. She glanced down at my protruding belly which was growing bigger by the day.

"It's finally your turn huh?" she asked with a laugh.

I grinned and nodded my head. "This is my mate Caspian," I introduced.

Reagan's eyes widened as she took in Caspian's face. She quickly schooled her face to neutral but by the way, Caspian ducked his head, I know he noticed the look of shock. He said he was used to that sort of thing happening, but I still knew it affected him.

"Hi Caspian, it's nice to meet you. I'm Reagan, the radiologist, let's go into my room and check out this baby, shall we?" Reagan said with a look that said she felt guilty for her slip up.

I didn't bother correcting her. It wasn't like she was trying to be cruel, it was an accident. It was hard not to be shocked when you first saw Caspian. One side of his face looked like it had completely melted. His right eye was sewed shut with skin that doctors had taken from his thigh. I wished there was more I could do for the scarring on his face, but it was still so raw and mangled that without literally cutting away the scarring, there wasn't a lot I could do.

I'd thought about asking Caspian if he wanted to see a plastic surgeon. To see if they could help, but I didn't know how to bring up the topic without him thinking I didn't like the way he looked. It didn't bother me that he had scars, hell, I didn't even notice half the time. But I knew how much it bothered Caspian.

"Alright, Burgess, lay up on the bed and lift your shirt," Reagan said. I laid up on the bed and lifted my shirt as she instructed. "You know what to expect."

I smiled and nodded as Reagan poured some of the cool gel onto my belly and then went ahead to use the wand to see the baby.

"Well, I can tell you that you are having twins," Reagan said.

My eyes widened and my head snapped to Caspian. "Twins? Are you sure?" I asked Reagan.

Reagan nodded her head. "Sure am," she said pointing at the screen. "There is baby A's heartbeat and there is baby B."

"Oh, my goodness, Iver never mentioned a second baby," I said turning back to Caspian who was smiling at me.

He chuckled and shook his head. "He might have mentioned something about it the other week when they came over."

"What?" I asked with wide eyes.

"He told me I wasn't allowed to tell you because the second baby wanted to be a surprise."

I barked out a laugh and shook my head. "Well, they got their surprise. Did he tell you what we were having?"

Caspian nodded his head. "Yep. Wanna know?"

"Oh wait, let me check the genders and we will see if Iver is right. Mind you he hasn't been wrong yet," Reagan chuckled. "Alright, got them. Let us know."

"He said that one is a boy, and the other is a girl, her name is Saffron she is a bison shifter," Caspian said before looking over at Reagan for confirmation.

Reagan laughed. "Well, I can't tell you what their name is or what kind of supernatural, but I can definitely tell you that you are indeed having a boy and a girl. I can also tell you that the girl is a lot bigger than the boy. But they are both extremely healthy and happy in there."

My mouth dropped open in shock as I blinked between Caspian and Reagan. "Thatcher and Saffron," I said as I played the names in my mind. At the same time, I watched on the screen as each baby gave a steady kick.

"I think they definitely like their names," Reagan said with a laugh.

I grinned. I couldn't be happier. But it did mean that all ideas I had for the nursery were going to need to change. I wasn't preparing for just one baby, we were preparing for two.

Chapter Eighteen

Caspian

I'd kept my promise to Iver that I wouldn't tell Burgess about the twins. The look on his face was priceless. It made me think about all the jokes and pranks I used to play on the guys at the firehouse. I wondered if Saffron was going to be like me. I hadn't been into the firehouse, but Jericho and I had been in constant contact since that first lunch at the Rigby family home.

It wasn't that I didn't want to go and see everyone. I was just scared. Going to the ultrasound appointment with Burgess had been terrifying enough. Reagan didn't know me, and she looked at me with such shock, I could only imagine what the guys I used to work with every day would do.

We were halfway through the pregnancy; Burgess had the weirdest cravings at the most inopportune times. He would want burgers cooked, using donuts as the bun. Just completely weird shit, but he would wake up out of a dead sleep at two in the morning to crave them.

I supposed it wasn't all that bad. He never got morning sickness and he never once complained about being pregnant. He loved every minute of it. He'd even started getting busy planning the baby nursery along with March. I'd seen some of March's artwork, it was gorgeous. With both their art on the walls the nursery would look amazing. That was all out of my element, I couldn't even draw a decent-looking stick figure.

It had been two weeks since we found out about the twins and Burgess was at work. I was sitting on the couch wondering what I was going to do with my life. I didn't want my kids to think all I could offer was being a sorry sack on the couch. I wanted more for them than that. I wanted to show them I could overcome. I just wasn't completely sure I could.

It had been a thought that had been playing on my mind for weeks. Probably since finding out that Burgess was pregnant. I wanted to do better. I wanted to be better. Dr. Carlisle had been shocked because I'd started sharing at the group therapy. It had been downright embarrassing to admit my weaknesses at the start, but once I got over that hump, I found it was easy to at least share something each week.

I could only thank Burgess for that. It had to be him. If the creator hadn't brought him into my life when they did, maybe I would never have progressed.

"Fuck it," I growled as I stood and slipped my boots on my feet, before bringing up the uber app. I still didn't drive. There was no reason I couldn't, other than the fact that I would have to be a bit warier with only having vision in one eye. But it was just something I wasn't ready to face yet.

It didn't take long before the uber pulled up out the front and I slid into the back seat.

"Caspian, you've been out and about a bit lately," Ryan laughed from the driver's seat. He was the same uber driver I always got. I liked him the most. He'd never looked at me like I was a freak.

"I'm healing," I said with a shrug.

"I'm proud of you man," he said with another smile.

The rest of the trip into Lalbert was spent chatting about the weather and whatever basketball team was sitting on top of the ladder. All the things that I no longer followed. I used to love all things sport. But then after the accident, everything I loved just got left behind.

Ryan pulled up in front of my old workplace. I took in a deep breath and glanced up at the large building, with its Perspex doors and bright red paint.

"Thanks, man," I said as I swung the back door open and slid out of the car. I shoved my hands down deep into my pockets and chewed on my lip as I agonized about going inside. It was one thing to be brave enough to actually come to the building but now I had to cross the threshold.

With another deep breath, I took the first steps towards a place that was like my second home only a short time ago. I reached out a trembling hand to the door and grasped it, swinging it a little harder than I'd expected. I could hear the voices of the guys out the back.

It was like going back in time. The scents, the sounds, and the feel of the place were still the same. It wrapped around me like a warm blanket, filling me with the comfort that I'd forgotten about. I'd wanted to be a firefighter since I was a child. I was so excited when I got accepted to be part of the Lalbert firehouse. It felt like forever ago.

I walked out towards where I knew all the guys would be goofing off, waiting for a call out. That was the beauty of Lalbert, there wasn't a whole lot that happened in the place. As soon as I stepped foot into the large garage where two red shiny trucks sat, I spotted Jericho.

He glanced up as I approached, and a broad smile crept over his face. He stood and widened his arms pulling me into a tight embrace.

"Caspian, man I'm so glad you finally made it," he said as he held me tightly against him.

I felt tears burning in my eye and I blinked hard as I sucked in a deep breath. "Thank you."

"Come on, let's go see the others, they've missed you."

I followed Jericho to the back of the garage where the other guys were sitting on milk crates at the back of the trucks. Some were on their phones while others had their legs kicked out in front of them with cups of coffee.

"Well, I'll be fucked," Maison said as he looked up and saw me. "Caspian. Fucking hell man, you are a sight for sore eyes."

Maison stood and hugged me tightly as the others all called out their greetings. I smiled and couldn't hold back the tears any longer that started to trek down over my cheek. They had once been my family and I rejected them. Yet here I was, like the prodigal son, feeling their love.

"Tell us everything you've been doing?" Kash asked as Maison let go of me and guided me to sit over on a milk crate.

I sat down and wiped the stray tears off my cheek. "Well, I'm mated," I started with a laugh at the wolf whistles.

"Fucking calm down, it's my brother he is mated to," Jericho growled.

That just caused more hooting and laughter as well as crude jokes. I found myself completely relaxing and falling into old times.

Chapter Nineteen

B urgess

"Okay now that you are having twins, what are the plans for the nursery?" March asked a week after finding out that we were expecting a little boy and girl.

"Would it be weird to do half and half?" I asked.

March chuckled. "Probably. Why not go gender-neutral?"

I hummed as I leaned back against the wall. We were sitting in the room that we were going to be turning into a nursery. Macklin and Caspian had pulled up and replaced the carpet with a plush beige color that would go with anything. The walls were painted white, but I wanted to turn it into a place of peace.

"Alright, let's do it this way. Close your eyes," March said. I flicked my eyes shut and waited for his next instructions. "I want you to envision little Thatcher and Saffron." I let my mind wander as I pictured a little boy with a shock of red hair, I didn't know if the vision was coming from the creator or if it was just my imagination, but the picture of Thatcher that I saw was a little boy with bright red hair and the most sparkling green eyes, almost the color of clover. The same laughter in his eyes that most fae had. Saffron would have dark hair, almost black, like Caspian's. Her eyes were the same hazel as mine.

"Now that you have them in your mind, I want you to ask them what they would envision for a peaceful place," March instructed.

No sooner had he finished speaking when a vision came to me. Suddenly I could see a large gnarled oak tree, woven with ivy. From the twisted branches hung a double swing seat. The sky was painted in pinks, purples, and blues, like a sunset in summer. The green grass looked as if it was swaying. In the trees were fae that seemed to dance amongst the branches. Mushrooms and toadstool grew among the grass and wildflowers.

I sucked in a deep breath and opened my eyes as I reached out for the sketch pad, I'd discarded in frustration earlier and started to sketch the picture in my mind. It didn't take me long and March didn't utter a word as I drew what I'd seen in my mind's eye. Once I was done, I sat back and looked down at the picture that had formed on the pad.

I glanced up at March who grinned at me. "This is beautiful. You know if you approached Maddox, he would be able to build a cradle that hung like a hammock."

My eyes widened and a grin split across my lips. I loved the sound of it. My fae and bison would live among their own enchanted forest. I nodded my head. "Yes. I want that. It's perfect."

March grinned. "It's because it is what your children wanted."

"Where did you learn to do that?" I asked.

March chuckled. "Iver. When I was pregnant with Ivy, I was so stressed that I would have the same thing that happened to Bear, and Iver was able to read it on me, so he showed me how to connect to Ivy's spirit."

I shook my head and laughed. "That kid. I always think I shouldn't be surprised when he does something amazing, yet it shocks me every time."

March nodded and grinned. "Me too. Come on let's go and see Maddox and then pick the kids up. They are desperate to spend some time with their Uncles Burgie and Casp."

I laughed and stood awkwardly as my belly was now huge. I couldn't believe how fast the babies were growing. I worried that I wouldn't have enough skin to stretch around them. Caspian loved my belly, he didn't keep his hands off it.

I was so proud of my mate. Since his trip to the firehouse, he had started to visit with the guys more regularly and get out there. He even mentioned that the captain was talking to him about working in the office. I thought it was a fantastic idea. Although Caspian couldn't go back in the field again, if he could work somehow with Lalbert Fire then it would be fantastic for him. He said that he would consider the offer but hadn't made up his mind.

March drove me out to where Maddox's workshop was set up. The panda shifter was an amazing artisan. His craftmanship was out of this world. Ever since I'd seen Iver's crib that he built I knew that I wanted something similar when I had children.

"Hey Burgess, March, good to see you both again," the omega greeted us with a friendly smile.

"Hey Maddox, how's it going?" I replied.

"Good, good, I've been busy out at the Devil's Advocate compound lately."

The Devil's Advocates had been busy building a school for the supernatural kids. I was still undecided whether we would be sending Thatcher and Saffron there. It was tempting to send them to the same school as their cousins.

"So, what brings the two of you here?" Maddox asked.

"I was hoping I'd be able to commission you to build me two cribs."

"Oh yeah, definitely. Do you have a design in mind?"

"Well, I was hoping you could build something that perhaps hung from the roof, a little like a swing or hammock."

Maddox's eyes widened and he grinned. "Okay, bear with me on this one, but you'll never believe it. So, two weeks ago, I swear I woke up in the middle of the night with this design in my head. I had to get up and draw it and then I spent last week building it because the design just wouldn't shake off me. Come and I'll show you."

I glanced at March who shrugged his shoulders. We followed Maddox out into the workshop, and I stopped dead as Maddox waved his hand towards the crib that hung from a frame. I looked at March with wide eyes who chuckled.

"That's exactly what I envisioned," I said quietly.

Maddox laughed and patted my back. "I had a feeling the right owner would come in. That was why I needed to make it so urgently. I'll make a second one for your other little one then."

I nodded my head and stared at the crib in silence. I couldn't believe it. The creator did work in peculiar ways.

Chapter Twenty

C aspian
"Stop looking at me like that," I said with laughter as I looked at Burgess.

"Like what? Like that you are a juicy peach that I want to sink my teeth into?" he asked with a touch of innocence.

I barked out a laugh. "Yes, exactly like that."

Burgess folded his arms across his huge belly and shook his head. "Now, why on earth would I want to stop looking at you like that?"

"Because I will want to do more than just get dressed and leave. I'll want to crawl back into bed with you."

Burgess grinned and stepped towards me, he opened his arms and wrapped them as best he could around my shoulders. His belly was squished between us.

"You are so damned handsome in that uniform, though," he laughed.

"It feels weird to be wearing it again. I sort of want to see myself in the mirror to see that it all fits."

"So, let's uncover the mirror and look," Burgess replied with a shrug.

It had been a long time since the accident. The scars on my chest, back, neck and arm were almost all covered in tattoos. But the scarring on my face, I knew was still horrible to look at. I wasn't sure that was something I was ever going to be able to face. I'd of course caught glimpses of myself in windows and reflective surfaces, but generally, I hadn't really seen myself.

I sighed as I weighed up whether or not I was brave enough to take this final step in my healing. I'd spoken to the Lalbert Fire Captain, Marlan. He offered me a job at the station. It wasn't going to be anything glamorous. It would be working the office, picking up calls, doing all the things that he normally did but really needed someone else to do. I'd thought it over for some time before finally agreeing.

I needed to start again. I needed to get out into the world and begin to live. Especially if I wanted to show my children that no matter what life threw at us, we could overcome. I looked into Burgess's face. I could tell that he wouldn't push me. That was how he was. He never pushed, he let me heal at my own pace. That's why I loved him.

Burgess chuckled. "Your face is going through a lot of emotions there."

I laughed and nodded my head. "Yeah."

"Wanna talk about them?"

I bit into my bottom lip and nodded again. "I love you."

The grin that took over Burgess's face lit up and made his eyes sparkle with delight. "I love you too."

I leaned forward and pressed my lips against his in a small but meaningful kiss. I'd never expected my life to turn out the way it did. Hell, if someone had said after my accident that I would have a mate who was expecting our first two children, I would have laughed in their face. But Mother fate did me a solid.

"Will you stand beside me while I look in the mirror?" I asked, still unsure whether this was the right decision to make.

"Always sweetheart," Burgess replied with a small smile. He reached out and took my hand before leading me into our bedroom where a large mirror had been taped over with newspaper. "Take your time and whenever you are ready, we can tear the paper off together."

I sucked in a deep breath and stared at the paper that was starting to curl at the edges and yellow with age. I could do this. I needed to do this. I couldn't go through life avoiding mirrors. I had to face what the fire had done to me.

"Okay," I said as I slowly reached up for a corner of the tape on one side of the mirror. Burgess reached for the other.

As soon as I started ripping the tape, I closed my eyes and listened as Burgess removed the tape on his side. The newspaper fell between us and the mirror, but I couldn't open my eyes. Burgess's hand tightened in mine, lending strength that I didn't have.

Very slowly I opened my left eye. My sight was blurry as tears formed on my lower lashes. With a swipe of my hand, I cleared my vision and gasped as I took in the damage done to my face. I knew that it was bad, from the way it felt, but nothing prepared me for what I would see. The scars were pink, in comparison to my naturally olive skin. The right side of my face appeared to have melted. My eyelid was sewn shut and waves of scarring rippled across my cheek.

"Fuck baby," I groaned as I took in the damage. "How can you even stand to look at me."

Tears started to trek down over my cheek as grief, pain, and hurt washed through me. I was a monster. My children would be afraid of me for sure. There was going to be no way that I could look them in the face.

Burgess released my hand and grasped my shoulders, turning me so that I was looking towards him.

"Caspian, I love you. I would love you not scarred, and I love you scarred. I can stand to look at you, because not only did Mother fate choose you for me, but I can see what a beautiful man you truly are. Your scars tell a story. They tell a story of a hero that went rushing into a burning house to save some children without fear. It tells a story of what kind of man you truly are that you were prepared to risk your life, your safety, and your body for complete strangers. I love you not because of the way the skin sits on your body, I love you because you are a hero, you love without expectation or condition. You honor me and treat me like a king. That is why I can stand to look at you. The scarring hurts me because it hurts you. But it never makes you ugly."

I pulled Burgess into my arms and pressed my lips to his. Burgess groaned against my mouth as my tongue swept past his teeth to tangle with his. I broke the kiss reluctantly and looked into the eyes of my mate.

"I love you, Burgess. More than all the words in the world can express."

Burgess smiled and pressed a quick peck to my lips. "I love you too, Caspian."

Chapter Twenty-One

Burgess

After kissing Caspian over and over before seeing him off on his first day at work I went into the nursery. March and I had laid down the undercoat and I was ready to make a start on the design. I'd organized to take time off from the shop, all my tattoo artists understood and promised to take care of things until after the babies were born and I was ready to get back to work. I wasn't sure that was ever going to happen. I loved my job, but the idea of staying home with my babies every day just seemed more appealing.

I'd pulled my pencils out to sketch first on the wall what I envisioned. March was dropping the kids off at the Devil's compound before joining me, we'd worked it so that we would each tackle a wall.

March had a very similar style in art to me so I trusted that he would be able to look at my sketches and complete my vision. I'd received a call from Maddox who said that the cradles were going to be ready in a few days, he was just doing some final touches. I was so excited. I couldn't wait to be able to meet my babies. I could just envision them in the room.

My family had gone wild in buying presents. Anghus, Bacchus, and Joachim had gifted us a changing table in a style similar to the cradles. Some of the Devil's Advocates had even got together to build a beautiful cabinet to keep the children's clothes in. It was branded with the Devil's Advocates symbol and runes that meant protection.

I rubbed over my belly as I glanced around the room with a smile on my face. "I can't wait to meet the two of you," I said quietly. "I know you will have a wonderful life here."

I heard the front door open and March call out to me as I stood in the center of the room looking at the sketches that dotted the walls.

"I have bought the whole store out of paint," March said with a laugh as he rounded the corner.

He stopped dead in the middle of the room and looked at the walls with wide eyes.

"Burgess, this is beautiful. It is so much better than I had even imagined."

I looked around the room with a smile. I could only imagine what it would look like once it was all done. Just the sketches alone looked exactly as my vision had been.

"I'm so happy with the way it's coming," I replied.

March nodded his head. "Asher gave me an idea last night and I wanted to ask you about it. We hadn't designed anything for the ceiling, but I was thinking, you wanted a sunset scene, so why don't we take that into the ceiling, we could also include small pin lights, so it looked like the roof was alive with lightning bugs."

I gasped and my eyes widened. "That is perfect. Do we know an electrician who could come and install it?"

March nodded. "Asher said there is a guy he knows through the club that is an electrician."

I laughed as I pulled my phone out of my pocket, ready to ring my brother. "Of course, he does."

March grinned. It was no secret in our family that Asher and March were a pair of kinky bastards.

"Burgess, I trust that you like the idea of the pin lights?" Asher answered my call.

I laughed. "I did. So, I hear you have a kinky electrician."

Asher chuckled. "I do indeed. His name is Ace Mattherson. He is an owner you could say."

I frowned. I'd long given up on understanding what the different kinks were. I liked the occasional slap on the butt during a hot sex session or dirty words, but I didn't share my brother's needs at all.

"I don't even know what that is, Asher," I said before quickly finishing. "And I don't want to know."

Asher barked out a laugh. "Okay. I won't tell you that he likes to own puppies."

"Jesus, Asher, I said I didn't want to know," I said with a laugh.

Asher chuckled. "Do you want me to text you his number or do you want me to organize for him to come out there and see you?"

"Yeah, just organize him to come out, it will be easier to explain my vision if he can see it."

"Can do. I'll give him a ring now and give him your number, he'll probably ring you to sort out a time to come around."

"Thanks, Asher, I really appreciate it."

"Anything for my little brother," Asher replied with a smile in his voice.

We ended our call and I looked over at March who was busy setting out tins of paint. "Ready to start our paint by numbers?" he said with a chuckle.

I laughed and nodded my head. "Let's do this."

Chapter Twenty-Two

Caspian

"Welcome back Casp," Captain Marlan Haldstedder greeted as I walked into the office.

I couldn't help the smile that crept over my face. My stomach was still in full flight with butterflies, but I was happy to be back. I felt like I'd found my home again.

Looking in the mirror that morning had been horrifying, but I was so grateful to have Burgess by my side. I didn't think I could do without him. We had worked fairly steadily on the tattoo that now covered most of my upper torso. I loved it. Not only were the scars hidden amongst the flames and the feathers of the phoenix, but I knew that it was done by my man.

"What will you need me to do?" I asked as I sat down opposite Marlan just as the phone rang.

"Well, you can answer that," Marlan said with a laugh.

I chuckled and picked up the phone. "Lalbert fire, how can I help?"

"Hello Lalbert fire, we have a house fire at 109 Newburt Road, the caller is on the line. Go ahead caller," the emergency operator stated.

I clicked on the computer and quickly started to input the address. "Just to confirm the address that is currently on fire is 109 Newburt Road, Lalbert?"

"Yes," a shaky voice said. They didn't sound much older than a teenager if that.

"Okay, and it is a house?"

"Yes. Please, hurry, there are people inside."

I sucked in a sharp breath. Déjà vu hit me all at once. "I've sent out a truck, it's coming to you now. How many people are trapped inside the building?"

"At least twelve," the caller said with tears in their voice.

"Shit," I muttered quietly. Captain Marlan had picked up the headset and was listening in to the call. He looked up at me and nodded his head in reassurance. I typed into the computer that there were twelve people possibly trapped inside, the computer would feed the information straight to Jericho and the team.

"How old are the people that are trapped?" I asked.

"I don't know. None of us know our age," the caller responded.

I glanced up at Captain Marlan who frowned and picked up the other receiver. "Kade Sinclair, this is Captain Marlan Haldstedder from Lalbert Fire, we have a potential crime scene at 109 Newburt Road. At least twelve people are trapped in a burning building, unknown ages, the caller just said they don't know how old they all are. Possibly a breeding facility."

I winced at the sound. "What is your name?"

"I don't have a name, they just call me Seven, because I was the seventh child born. Are the fire people coming?"

"Yes sweetheart, they are coming on their way, you are doing so good. Do you know how the fire started?"

"Yes, but I can't tell you, they will get in trouble."

"I promise that you won't be in trouble if you tell me," I reassured the child on the other end of the line.

"Five, he started it. He was angry at the keepers, they took nine away because they wanted to breed her but she was only small. She hadn't started her heats yet," Seven said.

"Seven, are you a boy or a girl?" I asked.

"I'm a girl. I'm a mermaid shifter."

"Where are the keepers now?" I questioned.

I glanced up at Marlan who was watching me and relaying everything that Seven said back to Kade from the AJE Authority.

"They were bleeding. Five, he went mad and cut them."

"And none of the other children have been able to get out of the building? Just you?"

"I don't know," Seven replied. "I can't see the house, the lady on the phone told me to find a street sign so I could tell her the letters."

"What are you using to ring me on?" I questioned, suddenly realizing that it was strange that this child would know how to use a phone.

"I stole one of the keeper's telephones, One put the number in the phone and told me to go out the front door and answer all the questions. I was to tell them the address, but I didn't know the address, it was the other lady on the phone that helped me."

I winced. I hoped that we were going to the right address. Captain Marlan must have been thinking the same thing as he quickly picked up the radio and called out to Jericho. Within seconds Jericho replied that they could see the smoke and they were heading in the right direction.

"You did such a good job Seven. Where are you standing now?"

"I'm on the corner of the street, the lady on the phone said for me to stand there until the fire people come. But I don't know what they look like."

I smiled. "They will be driving a big red truck." In the background, I could faintly hear the sirens and knew they were getting close. "Can you hear that loud noise?" I imitated the sound.

"Yes."

"That's the fire truck coming, when you see it, I want you to stay right where you are, don't go on the road or anything, just stay where you are, the firemen will go straight to the house and start putting out the fire."

"Okay, I can see it, it is coming down the road."

Sure enough, the sound of the siren was getting louder. I glanced up at Captain Marlan and he nodded his head.

"They've seen her, they've got the house."

The radio crackled as Jericho's voice sounded through. "We've got six kids standing out the front. Sending them all down to stand with the little girl on the corner. We will be going in to search for the others."

"Seven?"

"Yes," her little voice sounded.

"One of my firefighters, Jericho just told me that there are six kids that are standing out front of the house, they are going to come and stand down with you. When they get there, I want you to tell me which kids they are."

"Okay," Seven replied.

It was only a couple of minutes before I heard the crowd of kids chatting wildly.

"Five, One, Three, Nine, Twelve, and Eight are here," Seven said.

"Good job, there are going to be some people from the AJE Authority coming soon, they are going to help you too. They will probably be shifters and vampires, so don't be afraid when you see them."

"Okay. Can you talk to One, she is the biggest."

"Sure thing, you did a good job Seven," I said with a smile.

"Hello?" an older voice said through the phone.

"Hello, my name is Caspian, I'm with the Lalbert Fire, are you One?"

"Yes."

"How many other children were trapped inside the house?"

"There are three other children trapped and then two adults, but the adults are dead."

"Alright," I replied as Marlan radioed the information through Jericho and the team. "Do you know where in the house the three children are?"

"Yes, they will be in the basement, they will be locked in the cages."

Marlan's eyes were wide when he looked at me. I blinked my eye and my heart ricocheted against my chest. *What kind of fucking monsters were we dealing with?* Marlan informed Jericho of the information and we received affirmation that they were going down to the basement.

"There are adults here in white and blue cars," One said.

"Are they supernaturals? Shifters and vampires?"

"Yes. One is a vampire."

Marlan looked over at me and nodded. "Kade," he mouthed.

"Okay, One, they are with the AJE Authority, they are the police. They are going to help you all."

"So, we are safe now?" One asked.

"Yes, very safe. I'm going to let you hang up now so that you can talk to Kade, the big vampire. He is a good guy alright?"

"Okay. Thank you, Caspian," One said before the call dropped out.

The radio crackled again. "We've got three children, bringing them out now, all breathing but will need to be checked by medics," Jericho's voice said.

"Two adults upstairs, both deceased," Maison replied.

Just as One had told us. The two adults were killed by one of the kids. My stomach churned at the thought of what the hell these kids had just been put through. I couldn't even begin to think of the horrors they had faced.

Chapter Twenty-Three

Burgess

I was halfway through one wall when Ace knocked on the door. He wasn't anything like I had expected. Well to be honest I wasn't sure what to expect from a puppy owner.

"Hi there, I'm guessing you are Burgess?" he said. His smile was bright and gave him a youthful look. His bright blue eyes and stark blonde hair didn't scream dominant. Not that I even knew what dominant was supposed to look like.

"Yes, come on in and check out the room," I said with a smile as I waved Ace inside. He followed me down the hallway and into the nursery.

"Wow," he gasped as he took everything in. "These are going to be some very lucky babies that get to live in here."

I grinned and looked around the room. March and I had managed to get a good amount done.

"Hey Ace, good to see you," March said as he placed his paintbrush down on the tray.

"March, man you have some talent," Ace said as he still took in the room with wide eyes.

"I can't take credit for this. This was all Burgess. I'm just the lacky today."

Ace looked at me and I shrugged my shoulders. "March undersells himself. He is an amazing artist, I love having his work displayed in my shop."

"What kind of shop do you run?"

"A tattoo salon," I replied. "Shifter Ink."

"Oh, awesome. I've been meaning to get some more work done. Do you work on humans?"

I nodded my head and smiled. "Sure do. Some of our artists are humans too."

"I'll have to pop in. I'll wait until you've had the babies and back at work though, I think I want your work on me if this is the quality of your artwork."

I grinned. "I'd be honored."

Ace chuckled and shook his head. "No. I'd be honored. Now, tell me what you are thinking for the pin lights."

"I don't know how hard it will be, but I was hoping that I would be able to get pin lights across the ceiling, hardwired so that they have a switch of a night, to look like lightning bugs."

Ace glanced up at the ceiling and scratched at his chin. "Yeah, I can do that, but I will have to cut out the plaster on the roof and replaster. We will need to do that to hide the wiring."

I smiled and nodded. "That should be fine. The paint will be done in a couple of days, and we won't paint the ceiling until the new one is in."

"How long have you got left of the pregnancy?" Ace asked.

"Another two months."

Ace hummed and pulled his phone out. "I'm pretty booked out."

I felt my heart sink, I was hoping that he would be able to get it done before the babies were born, but if he couldn't I wouldn't make a fuss, it would be just something to do further down the line.

"I tell you what. Throw me in a discount on the tattoo and I'll call in a couple of my guys for the weekend, we will get it happening for you."

My eyes widened and I barked out a laugh. "I will give you your first tattoo on the house if you can get it happening over the weekend."

Ace stuck his hand out to me and shook mine. "Deal," he said with a smile before pressing his phone to his ear.

"Hey Dan, I've got a job for you and Mark over the weekend, a cashy job, if you want it," he said. I couldn't hear what Dan said in return but judging by the smile that Ace gave me it was going to go ahead.

My heart gave a leap with excitement. The room was coming up exactly as I was hoping. My babies were going to have the most amazing nursery.

"Alright, do you think the paint will be dry by Friday? There will be a bit of dust, taking down the plaster," Ace asked.

I nodded my head. "Yep, we should be finished painting by Wednesday and that will give it two days to dry. How long should it take to do the job?"

"It will take a few hours on Friday to get the plaster down, then Saturday, I'll be able to wire everything up. The plasterer will probably come in on Monday. It should be ready to paint by next Wednesday."

I grinned. That was perfect.

"Thank you so much, Ace, that is fantastic."

"Ah anything for Asher's little brother," Ace replied with a chuckle causing me to laugh.

Chapter Twenty-Four

Caspian

"You handled that call really well, son," Marlan said as I sat back in the seat and rubbed my hands up over my face.

My heart was still pounding in my chest. I couldn't stop thinking about the children, the trauma that they had already faced and were about to face further was just unbearable. I always hated calls involving children, I despised kids being hurt, but now as I was about to become a father the call struck me right in the gut.

"I just hope they will be okay," I sighed.

Marlan nodded his head. "Kade will make sure they get all the help they need."

"Yeah," I said as I leaned my elbows on the table in front of me. "I worry about what will happen to them, especially the one they called Five who killed the adults."

Marlan winced and nodded. "Yeah, that worries me too. But depending on the story will depend on what happens to them."

"Kept in fucking cages," I growled as I heard One's voice in my mind telling me about the three children that had been trapped in the basement.

"Yeah, it's fucking disgusting. What kind of sick cunt can do that sort of thing to a kid, I'll never understand."

"They need to fucking rot," I spat.

"Well, the ones that are dead will be rotting in hell now. Hopefully, they get tortured for eternity. I just hope they find the other child and whoever else is involved in this."

"Yeah, I hope so too."

"Alright, come on, let's go grab a cup of tea and relax for a moment, the boys will be back soon and will need to debrief," Marlan said as he stood from his seat and started to walk out the office towards the firehouse kitchen.

I stood and followed him. My mind was still firmly on the sound of Seven's voice. Such a young kid and terrified. There was going to be no way that my child would ever face such atrocities. I would give my life to keep them safe.

When the rest of the team arrived back, they all dragged themselves out of the truck and started the process of cleaning equipment and refilling what needed to be refilled.

"Man, I can live without ever fucking seeing that again," Kash said as he came into the lounge area and flopped down onto the couch.

"It sounded horrifying," I muttered as I sat in the chair opposite him. The other guys started to trickle in and set about getting themselves drinks or something to eat before joining us in the living area.

"You all, okay?" Marlan asked.

"If I have to see something like that again, it will be too fucking soon," Jericho growled.

"Alright, well let's debrief. What do you know?" Marlan asked looking around the room.

"The kids were all so fucking young. The eldest who they called One, would have been at the most seventeen I reckon. They didn't even know how old they were," Reign said as he shook his head in disgust.

"And the basement," Jericho said as he shuddered.

"There were three children there?" Marlan asked.

Jericho nodded his head. "The flames hadn't made it very deep into the house thankfully. The one that started it, Five, he was a phoenix shifter. He was able to create fire with magic. He'd not meant to set fire to the building, but lost control of his powers after he killed the adults."

"Who were they?" I asked.

"Kade said that they weren't known members of Morpheus," Jericho answered. Morpheus was a group of humans that took supernatural children and made them fight to the death for entertainment. "But it was definitely a breeding facility. Looking at the kids, they were all related. They were going to do DNA testing, but I would think that One was the mother of at least two or three of the kids."

"Do you know what happened to the child that they took away?" I asked.

"Kade was getting Onyx Rebels on it. Scout, one of the members had a good scent on them, so they were positive that they would be able to find the child," Jericho answered.

Everyone fell into a silence, getting lost in their own thoughts. I sent out a prayer to the creator that the child would be found.

"You guys did good," I said. "All of the children were saved. We can't change their pasts but at least now we know that their future will be somewhat brighter."

The guys nodded their heads. "Yep. Kade said he was going to be getting the kids the help they need. From what I could tell they would be taken to a halfway house with other omegas and then from there they would get therapy," Boston explained.

"That's good. They deserve some happiness in their lives now," I replied.

"Yeah, that's the least they deserve," Jericho answered.

I was glad that the call-out was the only major one for the day. I wasn't sure I would be able to cope with another harrowing call like that. The rest of the calls were for small issues, a little boy who got his hand caught in a bath drain and needed to get cut out, a minor car accident, and a kitchen fire at one local restaurant.

By the end of the day, I was looking forward to packing it in and heading home to my mate. I was physically and emotionally exhausted. But I felt good. I'd managed to achieve something that I thought I would never be able to face again.

Chapter Twenty-Five

Burgess

"This looks amazing baby," Caspian said as he looked around the nursery. The electricians and plasterers had done their jobs. March and I had spent the rest of the week painting the ceiling in a swathe of blues, pinks, and purples to make it look like dusk. The pin lights looked amazing. There was still one light bulb in the center of the room, but Ace had put the pin lights on a separate switch so both lights could be run individually.

"I'm so happy with the way it turned out," I said with a grin. "We are going to be getting the cradles tomorrow. Maddox already installed the hooks when the plasterers put the new ceiling in."

Caspian looked up at the hooks that sat in the beams in the ceiling that would hang our baby's cradles from. I was so excited to see them. I'd almost wanted to sneak into Maddox's workshop to get a preview, but I'd managed to contain myself and wait for the final piece.

Caspian stepped in behind me and ran his hands down over my belly. "I can't wait to meet our little man and lady."

I chuckled and leaned my back against Caspian. We only had just over a month to wait before they would arrive. My pregnancy had been a really easy one. I never once got morning sickness and I wasn't even getting a sore back or legs as March had got. I was lucky. I wasn't naïve to believe that all of my pregnancies would be this easy, but I was sure glad this one was.

Caspian pressed feather-light kisses against my neck. My eyes rolled in my head. One thing I did notice the more pregnant I got, the hornier I was. I could happily have Caspian's knot inside me constantly. I even considered getting myself a plug just to sit there. It was a strange feeling to just want to be completely filled.

He moved his fingers down over my belly to the hem of my shirt, before sliding his hands along my bare skin all the way to my nipples.

I gasped as his fingers pinched over the sensitive nubs that hardened under his touch.

Slick filled my boxers and my cock throbbed. Caspian continued to press kisses along my neck, nipping at the skin with his teeth, causing my eyes to roll in my head. I groaned and rocked my ass back against Caspian. His cock was hard. Reaching behind me I held onto Caspian's hips as I ground my ass against him.

"Want me to fill that little hole, baby?" he moaned.

"Yes," I gasped on a breathy sigh.

Caspian chuckled but removed his hands from under my shirt to take my hand in his and lead me into the bedroom. With frenzied movements, we undressed each other. It wasn't until we were both standing naked that our movements slowed back to the gentle passion that was building between us.

I lowered to my knees and leaned forward pressing my lips against Caspian's thigh. He reached down and threaded his fingers through my hair, holding on for purchase. I moved open-mouthed kisses up his thigh until I reached the apex of his legs. I ran my nose along the crease of his thighs, inhaling deeply, taking in the musk that was unique to Caspian.

I flicked my tongue over his balls, looking up at my mate through my lashes. Caspian's teeth sunk into his bottom lip as he watched me with a steely gaze. I opened my lips and sucked one of Caspian's balls into my mouth, swirling my tongue over the salty skin.

Caspian's fingers tightened in my hair as he jerked and moaned beneath my touch. I stroked over his cock, running my thumb over his slit, and gathering up the bead of pre-cum that oozed. Releasing his balls, I sat back on my knees and licked Caspian's pre-cum.

"I need to be inside you," Caspian moaned. He reached out his hand to take mine and helped me to stand. Leading me over to the bed, he laid me onto my back and lifted my ankles in his hands.

The scent of my slick filled the air between us, and my hole pulsed with need. Caspian ran his cock up and down my crease. My eyes rolled in my head with anticipation. I thought I was going to explode if he didn't push inside me soon. I fisted the sheets beneath me.

Slowly Caspian pushed himself inside me. The delicious stretch and burn had my toes curling and my cock giving a hard throb. I moaned and thrust my hips in the air as Caspian bottomed out.

He rocked back and forth, running the head of his cock over my prostate making me gasp and pushing me closer to the edge of my orgasm.

"Burgess," Caspian groaned as his movements sped up, he thrust into me like he couldn't get enough. I could feel his knot begin to grow inside me. It made Caspian's movements shallower, but the knot pushed hard on that pleasure button inside me.

I was gasping and moved my hand between us, grasping hold of my shaft I chased after that pleasure that was threatening to send me hurtling. With a few strokes, I felt my body begin to soar off the edge. I cried out as jets of cum sprayed against my stomach. Caspian roared in response and warmth filled me as he let go.

With a swift movement, he wrapped his arms around my back and twisted us, so that he was lying beneath me. I chuckled as I pressed my head against his chest.

"I love you, baby," he whispered as he kissed the top of my head.

"I love you too," I replied as I felt myself drifting off to sleep.

Chapter Twenty-Six

C aspian

I'd purposely come home early from work so that I could be there when Maddox arrived with the new cradles. I was as excited to see them as Burgess was. I hadn't been there to see the prototype but from what Caspian and March had described it was gorgeous.

The nursery was more than I could have even anticipated. Burgess and March had worked some kind of magic over the room. I could envision spending hours in there just watching our babies sleep or reading them stories.

The Rigby family didn't do anything by halves. They'd basically furnished the entire nursery and then some. I even overheard Anghus talking to Burgess about building a cubby house in the backyard for the kids when they were older.

I loved it. This was what family was supposed to be. It was something that I had missed out on growing up. I didn't have a safe place to call my own. That was something that was going to change in the next generation. The kids were going to know family, they were going to understand love and support.

Our children already had a sea of cousins just waiting for them to arrive. I'd joined Burgess on a trip out to the Devil's Advocates compound to see the school they had just finished building. The place was amazing. It was too early to make any real plans for where we would send the kids to school, but I loved the idea of them going to school on the compound and learning everything they needed to about being supernatural.

Just being with Burgess had taught me so much. There was a lot I had never been allowed to learn, but thankfully those around me were willing to show me and teach me. It meant a lot to me to have them by my side.

We'd discovered that the children who had been in the breeding facility that got burned were sent to live on the Devil's Advocates compound. They were now being adopted by two vampires, Larissa, and Corson. The kids were so happy. When Seven met me, she had practically climbed up into my arms and kissed my cheeks. There was no fear at all in her about my scars.

Anghus told us that the kids had been through hell. Jericho was right when he said that he believed One to be the mother of some of the children. As it turned out she was the mother of Seven and Five. I couldn't even begin to think of what it would be like to be forcibly bred for someone's sick gains.

Unfortunately, the AJE authority was never able to find Nine after she was taken. They believe that there was a chance that she was taken offshore and sold overseas. The sheer thought made me sick. I would hunt down and kill anyone that even considered hurting one of my children.

I was so glad to see that the children from this particular facility were growing and able to start overcoming what they had been through. Five was a strong alpha who was learning how to control his powers. Kade hadn't charged him with any crime, as it was self-defense. If it really was or not, we would never know, but it felt better to classify it as self-defense.

A knock on the door threw me out of my musings and when I opened the front door, Maddox was standing on the other side with a wide smile.

"Caspian, hi there. It's nice to finally meet you," he said as he stuck his hand out to shake mine.

"Maddox, it's great to meet you too."

Maddox smiled and nodded his head. "I'll go and grab the cradles and bring them in, then I can install them. Is this the last piece for the nursery?"

"It is, I can't wait to see them," I replied with a grin.

Maddox turned and went back to his truck bringing in two large boxes piled on a trolley.

"I'm so excited for this," Burgess grinned from beside me as he gave his hands a small clap.

I chuckled and threw my arm around my mate's shoulders and pressed a kiss to the top of his head.

Maddox wheeled the trolley with the boxes inside and towards the nursery before stopping just outside the door to lift the boxes off and carry each one inside the room. Burgess and I stood eagerly in the doorway watching as the panda shifter unboxed the first cradle.

I gasped as the beautifully and intricately made piece of furniture came out of the box.

"Maddox," I said with shock in my voice. "This is magnificent."

Maddox looked up at me with a grin and glanced over at Burgess. "I added a couple of finishing touches. This cradle is Thatcher's. I've carved in a fae at each end of the crib. On Saffron's, I've done the same with a bison. I just hope that Iver was right."

I laughed and nodded my head. "I know he is. He hasn't been wrong yet."

Maddox nodded. "So I've heard."

Maddox lifted Saffron's cradle out of the box he had it held in, and it was just as beautiful as the one that he'd made for Thatcher. I could just see my babies being in the cradles asleep.

"I'll go and grab my ladder and then we can hang them," Maddox said as he passed us and headed back towards his van.

"What do you think?" Burgess asked as he looked up into my face.

"They are more beautiful than I could have ever imagined. This whole room has completely blown me away. You really are so talented and amazing. You are going to make the best Papa that our children could ever ask for."

Burgess chuckled and shook his head. "I don't know, I reckon that you might make the best Dad that our children could ever ask for."

A goofy grin spread across my lips, and I kissed Burgess's lips with passion.

"Come on now, no more trying to make babies while you've still got two in your belly," Maddox said with a laugh as he came into the room with his ladder.

I pulled away from Burgess with a laugh. Maddox set out the ladder and then glanced over at me. "Can I get you to give me a hand to lift the cradle once I'm up the ladder?"

I nodded my head and walked into the center of the room. Once Maddox was on the top of the ladder, I lifted Thatcher's cradle with ease and handed Maddox each eyelet that was connected to the thick rope. He hung each eyelet to the hook.

"Alright you can let off the tension now," Maddox instructed.

I released my hold on the cradle and watched as it gently rocked side to side like a hammock.

"It's perfect," I gushed.

Maddox grinned. "I'm really glad I got the opportunity to do this for you both. Your children are really going to be blessed."

I looked between Maddox and Burgess with a grin. It was true. Our children were not only going to be blessed but were a blessing to us.

Caspian

I was useless. I felt so helpless. My mate was in so much pain. His face was red and screwed up. Tears leaked from the corner of his eyes as Dr. Osbourne sat on a stool between Burgess's legs.

"Alright, Burgess one more push and baby number one will be here," Dr. Osbourne instructed.

Burgess gritted his teeth and clasped my hand in a vice grip as he pushed with all of his strength. He cried through grit teeth. I looked down between Burgess's legs in time to see a beautiful red-haired baby come into the world. The baby let out a loud shriek as Dr. Osbourne twisted him in his hands.

"Your baby boy is here," Dr. Osbourne said as he lifted our son to Burgess's chest.

"Oh baby," Burgess cried as he looked down at the baby. I was in awe. Burgess had never looked more beautiful to me.

"Caspian, do you want to cut the cord?" Dr. Osbourne asked.

I turned to him with a grin and nodded my head. Dr. Osbourne handed me a pair of surgical scissors and pointed to the area I was to cut. With a quick snip, our son was released from his cord and was snuggled into Burgess's chest.

"We just need to deliver the placenta and then when you feel the urge to push again it will be time for the little girl to come into the world," Dr. Osbourne said. But his voice was lost as I stared down at my son.

"Thatcher," I said with a smile.

Burgess looked up at me with an exhausted grin. "He is beautiful."

I nodded my head. "Like his Papa." It was true. Thatcher was the spitting image of Burgess, from the red hair to the little button nose.

"Not all me. Look at those green eyes. They are definitely you."

I looked down closer at my son and when he looked up at me, I could have sworn that he smiled. He kept his eyes connected to mine. Burgess was right, Thatcher had the greenest eyes. They played with mischief which told me he was most definitely fae.

"Oh god, I have to push again," Burgess groaned.

"Alright, let me take your little man so that you can concentrate on birthing your daughter," the nurse said as she took Thatcher and wrapped him in a blanket, and placed him in a crib.

It was as if Thatcher knew that he was only being handed off to the nurse so that his sister could enter the world. He didn't make a peep, instead seemed quite content to look around the room.

I took Burgess's hand in mine once more as he bared down. His teeth were grit and he cried out again.

"She is crowning, so on the next push, give us a big one and her head will be out," Dr. Osbourne instructed.

Burgess didn't say anything but nodded his head. Within seconds he squeezed my hand tight and roared as he pushed once more. I looked down between his legs to see our daughter's dark hair enter the world.

"Okay, no pushing for a second, so I can check the cord," Dr. Osbourne said.

Burgess breathed heavily until he was given the go-ahead to give another push. With the next push, our daughter fell into the doctor's arms with the identical squawk that her brother had given.

Dr. Osbourne placed Saffron on Burgess's chest. She was the polar opposite of Thatcher. Her dark hair was almost black. And when she looked up at me her hazel eyes were the same as Burgess.

"Beautiful girl," I said quietly as I ran my finger down over her cheek.

Tears welled up in my eye as I looked down at my daughter and then back over at my son. I had been truly blessed, in a way that I never thought was possible. Saffron reached out a pudgy hand and circled her fingers around mine.

"She already loves her Daddy," Burgess said.

"I love her so much, I love Thatcher so much. I'm in awe," I said reverently.

"Alright, Caspian, ready to cut the cord for your daughter?" Dr. Osbourne interrupted. I smiled and nodded again as I repeated the process of cutting the cord for Saffron. Once it was done, I turned back to Burgess with a smile.

Burgess looked up at me and grinned.

"I'm so proud of you, baby. You are a superstar," I said as I leaned down and pressed a kiss to Burgess's lips.

"I would do it over and over to have these babies in my arm," he said as he kissed the top of Saffron's head.

"I'm going to just give little miss a check over and then I'll bring her back," the nurse said as she wrapped Saffron in a warm blanket and took her over to a cradle. The other nurse brought Thatcher back and laid him on Burgess's chest.

Thatcher looked up at his Papa and his eyes danced with delight. This was my life. Our life. I couldn't believe just how fortunate we could possibly be. My children. I would protect them with my dying breath to make sure they grew up to have everything they needed in life.

The End.

Don't miss out!

Visit the website below and you can sign up to receive emails whenever S L Davies publishes a new book. There's no charge and no obligation.

https://books2read.com/r/B-A-NZRR-IDFBC

BOOKS 2 READ

Connecting independent readers to independent writers.

Also by S L Davies

Breeding Facility
Memphis
Bacchus
Coltrane
Pax
Raiden
Nash

Devil's Advocates
Lynx
Israel
Jai
Jasper
Arley
Zion
Oakland

KINK
Freya
Tanquil

Obsidian Mechanics
Donte

Onyx Rebels
Onyx Rebels Prologue
Hawke

Rigby Brothers
Asher
Burgess

Schiavu
Schiavu

Standalone
Sisters Revenge
Killer Love
Soldiers At War
Second Chances
Bunny
Caged

Watch for more at https://www.amazon.com/~/e/B0832T8F7Z.

About the Author

S L Davies is an Australian Author living in Country, Victoria. She is inspired by the world around her.

Read more at https://www.amazon.com/~/e/B0832T8F7Z.